Falling in Love on Route 66

A Brother's Best Friend Romance

Kaci Rose

Five Little Roses Publishing

Copyright

or to businesses, companies,
events, institutions, or locales is completely coincidental.

Book Cover By: **Cover Girl Design**
Editing By: Debbe @ **On The Page, Author and PA Services**
Proofread By: Ashley @ **Geeky Girl Author Services**

Contents

Get Free Books!

Do you like Military Men? Best friends brothers?
What about sweet, sexy, and addicting books?

If you join Kaci Rose's Newsletter you get these books free!

https://www.kacirose.com/free-books/
Now on to the story!

Chapter 1

Rory

Of course, my brother decided to get married on the other side of the country. His soon-to-be wife wants a Napa Valley wedding. I can't blame them because what she is planning looks beautiful.

Plus, this is the perfect opportunity to cross off one of my bucket lists items. Road tripping down Route 66! I live in Chicago, which is the start of Route 66, and my brother's wedding is a few hours north of the end of Route 66.

While Napa Valley is six and half hours north of the end of Route 66, according to my map app, it's still the perfect chance to make the drive. I have plenty of vacation time saved up at work and have it planned just right to take me two weeks to get out there.

That still gives me enough time to help with any pre-wedding stuff and fly home after the wedding while still having a few days to settle in before going back to work. My parents are already out there spending time with their soon-to-be daughter-in-law and her family, so with everything to be done, it will also keep my brother busy until then.

I'm feeling really good about this trip until my brother calls.

"So, you are really going through with this two-week road trip?" Nate asks.

"Yes, I told you I am. My time off from work has been approved, and everything's set."

"Well, I don't want you making this trip alone."

"I'll be fine. Besides, don't you think it's a little late to find someone to go with me?"

I'm supposed to be leaving in a few days, and there is no way I'm changing my plans now.

"That's why Weston is going with you," he says

"What? Are you serious? I'm sure he has better things to do than babysit me," I groan.

Weston is my brother's best friend. They met on the first day of kindergarten and have been friends ever since.

Growing up, I had such a crush on Weston, but he's always been off-limits, older brother's best friend and all that. Though I haven't seen much of him in the last few years since I went away to school and moved into the city.

"He works from home, and he agreed you shouldn't be making that drive alone. It's already a done deal. He'll pick you up Monday morning."

"I wanted to do this by myself!"

"And I want you to be safe. Traveling across the county alone isn't safe. You know that as well as I do. He promised to abide by whatever road trip rules you set."

"Fine, Nate. But if he ruins this for me, you're paying for a do over."

My brother made this app that helps with grocery shopping, sales, and coupons. I don't know the details, but I do know he sold it to a major grocery store chain for millions of dollars and doesn't have to work a day in his life now. But he's also working on another app now, and I doubt he will stop working. He loves creating things.

"Deal. But he isn't going to ruin this for you. Just be nice to him, okay? He's doing this as a favor to me."

"Yeah, sure 'cause every girl dreams of being a charity case," I grumble.

He spends the next half hour talking wedding stuff with me as I finish packing and sorting out my stuff.

When I get off the phone with Nate, I call my best friend Kinsley and tell her what Nate pulled. She knows how I felt about Weston all those years ago and how I still crush on him when I see him at family functions.

The last time I was over at her place, we had too much wine and stalked his social media going back a few years. He doesn't seem to have had a girlfriend in a while, or he was good at deleting everything once they broke up.

"Just think, you'll have someone to carry your bags, and he can drive while you get to enjoy the scenery. Plus, it can't hurt to have some eye candy on your trip, and if you end up in bed, all the better," she says.

"Kinsley! I would never!"

"Why not? He's hot and gives off a bad boy vibe, so I'm sure he's good in bed. You haven't been with anyone in what? Six months? Have a vacation fling, and then go your separate ways after the wedding. No one ever has to know."

"He's my brother's best friend. I have to see him at family events!"

"So? Maybe you can be friends with benefits and hook up at family stuff." I can imagine her wagging her eyebrows as we speak.

"Just no," I say as my call waiting goes off. "Speak of the devil, Weston is calling me. I got to go."

"Just think about it!" She says before hanging up.

"Hey West," I answer and try to push Kinsley's remarks out of my head.

"You, okay?" He asks in his dark, giving me shivers voice.

"Yes, I was on the other line with Kinsley, and she is trying to convince me to do all sorts of things on my trip."

"Yes, I heard I'm taking you on a road trip?"

"You don't have to, you know. I had plans to make this trip on my own."

"Nonnegotiable. A beautiful young woman like yourself alone is just asking for trouble."

Did he just call me beautiful? No, I push it out of my head. I'm not going to overthink this.

"Yes, you're going to have to go along with my plans. We'll drive Route 66, make lots of stops, and eat lots of junk food. You're going to have to smile in pictures too."

"I'm looking forward to it."

"Liar."

"Well, we always had fun, didn't we? Why wouldn't we have fun on a road trip together?"

"I guess."

"See you Monday, Rory."

At least I'll get a break at night when we go to our own rooms.

I can do this. I won't let him ruin the trip.

Two weeks in a small, confined space with the hottest guy I've ever known?

This isn't going to end well.

***

Weston

What the hell was Nate thinking? Asking me to drive across the country with his sister?

How many times did he warn me to stay away from her when we were growing up?

More than I can count, that's for sure. I tried to hide how much I liked her growing up and failed at it. Nate would catch me watching her and then give me an entire speech about how his sister is off-limits.

My feelings toward Rory haven't changed. I might have gotten better at hiding it, but having me driving across the country with her for two weeks to his wedding in one of the most romantic spots in the country just doesn't seem like a good idea.

He seemed to have a comeback for every excuse I had. The one that still shakes me is he trusts me with her and knows I won't let anything happen to her.

Damn right, I won't let anything happen to this girl.

Still, I feel it in my gut that this is a bad idea. My best friend's sister and the girl I have crushed on for years happens to be the one I can't touch.

All that being said, I can't help but be excited about this trip. After all, it is two weeks alone with a woman who I consider a friend.

We have always had a great time together. Though most of the time, she was tagging along with her brother, and I didn't mind. Rory was always a lot of fun and skilled at getting us out of the trouble Nate got us into.

That's what I tell myself as I knock on her door a good twenty minutes early. But when she opens the door, clearly flustered, the smile falls from my face. Her light brown hair is pulled up in a messy bun, and she's in jean shorts and a t-shirt. Her tan legs are on display, and she looks beautiful but still comfortable enough for a road trip.

"What's wrong?" I ask, ready to jump in and help fix it.

"Since we're driving and have 'so much extra room,'" she uses air quotes around the last part. "Nate gave me a list of shit to bring since he's moving there. I guess it's stuff he left here when he moved out."

"Well, that explains why he insisted I rent an SUV to drive us out there. What's going? I'll start loading it up."

She points to a few boxes by the door, so I start there. By the time the boxes are loaded, she has her bags ready to go and seems calmer.

Thirty minutes later, we are finally on the road, and she's relaxed slightly, but not much. She seems still a bit on edge, but I want her calm and enjoying the trip.

"What's our first stop? You are in charge." I ask, thinking maybe if I can get her mind back on the trip she'll relax and enjoy it.

Growing up, I can remember her talking about driving Route 66. She even had a book of stops and things she wanted to do on the drive.

"I figure we can stop in St. Louis tonight. That's four hours of driving and gives us plenty of time to stop along the way. There are a few places I'd like to see," she says.

Then she plugs the first stop into the GPS, shifting so she's leaning against the door.

Finally, her posture is much more relaxed. After I put on some music and then after our first photo stop, she seems to be loosening up and enjoying the drive.

"So, we have to stop at the Cozy Dog Drive-in for lunch," she says.

"Isn't that where the corn dog was invented?" I ask.

"Yes!" A huge smile lights up her face as she starts to bounce in her seat.

That smile is going to do me in because I know there isn't anything I won't do to keep it there over the next two weeks.

We get our lunch, and she makes sure to order something different from me, and we try each other's food. I was never really a fan of sharing food, but with her, it's easy and natural.

Day one, and I'm already falling down a dangerous slope.

After lunch, we hit the Pink Elephant Antique Mall, and I follow behind her as she walks through rows and rows of things for sale. Watching her bend over to look at items is driving me crazy. With the bottom swell of her beautifully round ass cheek peeking out of these cut-off shorts, I'm trying to tamp down a hard-on.

If I want to keep my cock in check, I'll have to keep my eyes diverted. The last thing I need to do is make things uncomfortable from day one. Plus, I'm sure there is no way she feels the same way about me.

I'm sure she sees me as another annoying older brother, especially after being forced with me on this trip.

But I'm a glutton for punishment, so I still walk behind her and watch the way her hips sway down the aisles.

When we get back to the car and on the road, I breathe a sigh of relief. As we near St. Louis, she turns down the radio.

"I was thinking we'd go visit the Gateway Arch, then grab dinner and head to the hotel?" She asks like I'm going to tell her no.

This is her trip, and pretty much anything she wants to do, we'll do, assuming it's not going to put her in harm's way. If she wants to visit the Gateway Arch, then we'll visit. If she wants to bungee jump off the Arch, that's where I'll put my foot down.

The smile I love is back as we ride to the top of the Gateway Arch. It's just the two of us in our pod on the ride to the top. While we are sitting on opposite sides, her leg keeps brushing against mine, and it's causing some sparks, making my heart race.

"You, okay?" She gives me a funny look.

I'm a big guy as it is, and while this pod might have five seats in it, I can't imagine if there were three other people with us. It's tight enough with just us here. So, I go with that as my excuse.

"Yeah, I think it's just the small space," I tell her because she doesn't need to know that it's her who is affecting me like this.

That was the wrong thing to say because she moves to sit beside me and wraps her arms around mine.

"It's okay, I'm right here with you. After this, I promise no more small spaces. I didn't realize they bothered you."

"No, we are not changing your plans. I can handle tight spaces, I promise. It's easier with you here."

While I know this is a dangerous road, but if the small spaces get her pressed up to me like this, I'm all for them. Even though I shouldn't be.

At the top, we take photos and enjoy the view. I'm looking out over the water when one of the old riverboats glides by. It goes at a slow, lazy speed, almost like it's reminding me to slow down and enjoy this trip. I'm going to have two weeks with Rory.

Two weeks of just us. I'm going to enjoy it while it lasts.

Chapter 2

Rory

Weston insisted on checking us in at the hotel, and I let him. With him, I know I need to pick my battles, and something small like who checks us in isn't a battle I want to fight.

He comes back out, helping me with the bags. When we walk back through the lobby to the elevators, he presses the right floor and then looks over at me.

"Here's your room key," he says.

Taking the plastic card from him, I check the room number. Then I walk down the hall and stop in front of my door. Looking back, I can see he's watching me, and I assume he wants to make sure I get into my room and lock the door. So I open the door and step in.

It's a pretty standard hotel room with two beds. What I don't expect is for him to step into the room behind me.

"Hey, excuse you! Why do you think you can barge into my room?"

"Our room."

It takes a minute for what he said to sink in. Did he just say *our* room?

"No way! We are not sharing a room. Why do you think we need to share a room?"

"We are because it's too dangerous for you to be on your own."

He sets his bag down on the bed closest to the door. Always the protector. I want to smile because my dad did the same thing when we traveled. He and my brother took the bed closest to the door, and my mom and I shared the other one.

"Nope, not going to happen. I didn't agree to this, and my sleep clothes are completely inappropriate to be in around you. Furthermore, I'm not sharing a bathroom with you." I cross my arms over my chest, suddenly uncomfortable as his eyes rack down my body.

When his eyes land back on mine, he smirks.

"I can put the seat down," he says and pulls out clothes and other things to take a shower.

"Not the point," I sigh. After tonight, he will get two hotel rooms, and I'll just have to prove my point.

Once he's in the bathroom, I sit on the bed, pull out my phone, and text my brother.

Me: I did NOT agree to share a room with him!!!

Nate: I know, but it's the safest. If someone knows you are sleeping alone, they might try to break in.

Me: Why are you so paranoid? Did you join the mafia?

Nate: No, but Mandy watches those true crime shows, and it has made me more aware.

Me: Tell her this is all her fault and whatever happens is her fault.

Nate: See you in a few weeks. Love you.

Me: Love you too, barely.

I have never had a problem with Mandy, Nate's fiancé, and my soon-to-be sister-in-law. But if she is making him this paranoid, we need to have a talk.

Since the shower is still running, I decide to call Kinsley.

She answers on the first ring, so I know she was waiting for my call.

"How goes the road trip with Westie the Hottie?" she giggles.

"Good lord Kins, what if he was standing right here?"

"Is he?"

"No, he's in the shower because he's insisting we share a room because it's too dangerous for me to have my own room."

"What?!" she screeches.

"Yeah, apparently Mandy is a true crime junkie and freaked my brother out, so my brother insisted."

"Figures. He's always been super overprotective," she says.

Kinsley and I met our freshman year of college, and even then, my brother was still protective. She found it funny, but I was annoyed. Until now, he had mellowed out, but I won't put up with him starting up again.

"Yeah, this is only day one."

"Well, how was the rest of the day?"

"It was actually pretty pleasant. You were right. It was nice to have someone else drive while I just enjoyed it."

"See, I don't think this trip will be that bad. Now let me tell you what happened at my sister's work today."

She goes on talking about her twin sister's boss when the shower turns off. A moment later, the bathroom door opens, and out walks Weston in nothing but a towel.

What the hell?

He was always in shape in school from playing sports, but I didn't need to know he's kept in even better shape. Holy hell, those are some abs. I watch a drop of water slide over his hard nipple and ripple over each ab until it moves through his happy trail and is soaked up by the towel.

"Rory, are you still there?"

"I'm going to have to call you back," I say and hang up without waiting for a response.

"Why didn't you get dressed in there?"

"I forgot my boxers. I'm not used to sharing my space either," he shrugs.

Great, this isn't going to be as easy as I had hoped to hide my feelings. When he goes back into the bathroom, I get my stuff ready to take a shower.

"Your turn," he smiles when he walks out again. I don't say a word as I grab my stuff and head into the bathroom.

The hot water from the shower feels good. I didn't realize how tense I was from having my high school crush sitting next to me all day, not to mention him walking out of the bathroom in nothing but a towel.

Who does that?

Oh well, I'll get dressed, go right to my bed, and get under my covers. Maybe we can watch some TV and that will be the end of this. Once he sees how inappropriate my sleep clothes are, next time he'll want his own room.

As I put on my sleep clothes, I figure I might need to stop and get something more, well more, to sleep in. My tank top, with no bra and tiny cotton shorts, really is not appropriate around Weston.

When I packed, I wasn't planning on his tagging along, and even once I knew he was, I thought we'd have separate rooms at least. It never crossed my mind to pack something more modest. I like to be comfortable.

There is nothing I can do about that now, so taking a deep breath, I step out of the bathroom.

Weston is sitting on his bed shirtless in a pair of black basketball shorts, with his back against the headboard.

When he looks up from his phone, he groans.

"I see your point. But still no separate rooms," he says.

Shrugging, I smile sweetly, "I'm surprised your girlfriend is okay with you sharing a room with another girl." Then I put my dirty clothes away and get into bed.

"No girlfriend, and I know you don't have a boyfriend, so don't even try to play that card."

"How do you know I'm not seeing someone?"

"Because I'm on your social media, and Kinsley is friends with my sister, and they talk."

"She has a big mouth," I grumble.

"Want to watch some TV before bed?" he asks.

"Sure."

I don't think either of us knows what we're watching, but it was a good enough distraction.

***

Weston

We have been on the road now for a few days, and other than Rory's revealing nightclothes, things have been easy. We are talking, and she's more relaxed. It's what I had hoped would happen.

I want her to have fun and enjoy this trip. Watching her experience it has been enjoyable for me. The way she lights up is when she gets to see something that had been on her wish list for a while captures my heart.

She has pulled me into more photos than I'd like, but for her, I'll do it.

It's no different today as she climbs into the car and we get on the road.

"What's the plan today?" I ask.

"The Blue Whale!" she says. Her eyes alight with anticipation.

"That one I've been looking forward to as well. Where is our stopping point today?"

"Oklahoma City."

I nod in agreement because she's been great at planning the stops. She allows plenty of time for us to get out of the car or to eat lunch. I like the pace she has set because we aren't rushed, and we get into our stopping points about dinner time so there haven't been any late nights.

Really, it seems like she could have made this trip alone, as she's very responsible. She isn't some out-of-control party girl, but I won't tell her or her brother that. I like being here with her, and this experience is not something I would have wanted to have passed up.

She rolls down the windows, cranks up the music, and starts singing along as we cruise down an open stretch of highway. I can't wipe the smile off my face because this girl is beside me, happy and exuberant, and really, that's all I've ever wanted for her.

As we get closer to the Blue Whale, she starts giving me directions from her phone. When we get to the parking lot, I'm relieved to see we are the only people here. I guess it helps it's a workday, and we are here pretty early.

As we get out, I take in the cute little park by the water. Had we known, it would have been a great place to have a picnic.

"Come on, slowpoke," Rory says as she loops her arm in mine and almost drags me toward the faded blue whale.

It kind of looks like it's made from paper mâché, similar to the projects we had to make in school. It sticks out into the water, and we're able to walk through it all the way to the end of its tail, which is over the water.

"Oh, I love this! We have to get some photos!" She says, skipping off ahead of me.

I walk slower than she does, but it's because I like hanging back and watching her experience things, seeing how her face lights up, and enjoying her gorgeous body. Though I'm also trying to find the best spot for a photo.

She disappears into the whale and a moment later appears at the top with her head out one of the holes by the whale's nose.

"Wait, let me get a picture!" I call as I pull out my phone.

She strikes a pose for the photo with a huge smile on her face. I snap a few more, then turn and take a selfie with her in the background. That's the one I send to Nate.

Me: She's loving this stop.
Nate: I can tell. That was one she would always talk about. I'm glad she is getting to see it. How's the trip going?
Me: Good. Though she's still mad about the one-room thing, but otherwise, it's actually been fun.

"Get your nose off the phone and experience this!" Rory calls from the whale's mouth.

"I just sent that photo to your brother!" I call back.

When I finally walk through the whale's mouth and further in to get in the shade, she's already down by the whale's tail.

"Look, there is a platform to climb for photos," she says, coming over to position her phone on one of the ledges, then taking my hand and dragging me with her.

"How are you taking a photo?" I ask.

Holding up the pen from her phone, she smiles. I just shake my head. She likes those fancy phones.

After posing with me and snapping some photos, she jumps down and checks her phone.

Standing, I just look over the water. I want to soak up this moment with just the two of us and how happy she is. Then she joins me and we both lean on the edge looking over the water.

"Thank you for coming with me on this trip," she says, shocking me. "It's been more fun than I expected having someone with which to share the experience."

"I've been enjoying myself. This isn't a trip I would have taken on my own, but I'm glad I'm here."

When I look down at her, she's closer than I realize. She looks up at me, and her warm brown eyes are sparkling. Her stare pulls me in, and I'm frozen in place and couldn't move if I tried.

She reaches up and tucks a piece of her hair behind her ear, and that simple move has me hard. Who knew that was even possible? Yet when she licks her lips, I'm done for. There is no way I'm not going to kiss this girl.

My eyes move to her lips, and like we are two magnets which don't have a choice, we're drawn to each other.

I reach up and tuck another piece of hair behind her ear but don't pull my hand away as I lean down and our lips meet.

The kiss is soft as our lips barely touch, but then she melts into me, and I deepen the kiss without a second thought. This is the kiss I dreamed of growing up, and to be here in the moment feels surreal.

She tastes like strawberries, and her lips are so much softer than I expected.

I'm lost in the kiss until she moans, then reality seeps back in. This isn't any girl, this is Rory. I pull back, but the sight of her head tilted up to me, eyes closed, and lips parted is too tempting.

So, I place another soft kiss on her lips before stepping back and putting space between us.

Her eyes open, and she looks at me. Neither of us says a word as she smiles and turns to head back to the car. I run my hand over my face. My emotions are so confusing.

As I turn to follow her, my thoughts start to go to war. I can't touch her. She's Nate's sister, but she is the girl I've crushed on almost all my life. I can just enjoy these two weeks with her and see how it goes, right? It's probably a simple schoolboy crush that will burn out before we even hit California.

Let's hope Nate doesn't find out.

Chapter 3

Rory

Holy Hell! Weston kissed me. I mean, he really KISSED me. We haven't said a word to each other since and have been on the road for an hour, and will be getting into Oklahoma City soon.

The time passes in a blur as I keep thinking about that kiss and every move he made. I realize we're at the hotel until he shuts off the car. When I look over at him, he's looking at me too.

Still, we say nothing as we grab our bags and go check-in.

It isn't until we get to our room that he finally breaks the silence between us. He sets his bag down on the bed and looks at me.

"We should talk about it," he says exactly as I expected him to.

That's when I have to know if he regrets it. I don't think I could handle it if he does. If he says it can't happen again, I'm all right with that, but I can't stand him regretting it. I'm not sure where the boldness comes from, but before I can second guess myself, I'm asking him the question.

"Do you regret the kiss?"

"Hell no," he says with such certainty.

It's almost like he's mad at the thought that he could possibly regret it.

I nod, lost in thought. How did I feel about it? That's what I've been trying to figure out. I may not know for sure, but I know one thing.

"Good, neither do I," I tell him.

"Yeah?" he asks as his eyes stay on me, and he takes a tentative step toward me.

I don't break eye contact, and before I know it, he's standing right in front of me.

"Yeah," I confirm, and that's all he needs before his lips are on mine again.

His hand cradles the back of my head, pulling me to him, and I'm learning the feel of his lips on mine. His other hand grips me, pulling me impossibly closer before sliding around to my lower back and gripping me tight against him.

It's as if he wants to get as close as he possibly can, which works for me as I'm enjoying every moment of it. With him this close I can feel his hard dick pressing into me. When he angles my face to deepen the kiss, I groan.

The moment my lips part, his tongue is on mine, and his hand runs up my back and up my neck to cup my face. This kiss is everything. It's more intense than the one we had at the Blue Whale earlier today.

His lips are possessive, and this kiss is staking a claim, and I'm letting him. There is nothing I want more than to be his. I run my hands through his hair as he continues to possess my mouth.

He only pulls away when we need air and rests his forehead on mine as we catch our breath.

"This isn't just a vacation fling for me," he whispers and places his hand on my shoulder like he is going to stop me from running.

My heart soars. He's not satisfied and wants more, which makes me elated because that's exactly what I want too.

"Good me either," I whisper, still trying to catch my breath.

He reaches up and gently cups my face.

"Then I'm taking you to dinner tonight as a date. I'm going to do this right," he says.

"Okay." I barely whisper.

He leans down and gives me another chaste kiss before pulling back.

"Go get ready," he tilts his head toward the bathroom.

I get my nicest dress, the one I had planned to wear to the rehearsal dinner, grab my phone, and go to the bathroom.

I lean against the closed door and squeeze my eyes shut.

Holy shit! Weston kissed me twice!

I put my phone on silent and then text Kinsley.

Me: Weston kissed me!!!
Kinsley: What?!
Me: Twice
Kinsley: You're serious?
Me: Yes, and he's taking me on a date tonight!
Kinsley: You better not be joking, or I'll kill you!!
Me: I swear it! You can't tell ANYONE. My brother needs to hear this from me.
Kinsley: I won't say a word because I agree he should hear it from you.
Me: AHHH! I have to get ready for our DATE!
Kinsley: I want all the details!
Me: Promise!

I set my phone down and take a deep breath. I hadn't planned to go on any dates on this trip. The only two nice dresses I have are this one and a sexier outfit for the bachelorette party.

I can spice the dress up by doing my hair and makeup, so I get to work.

Less than twenty minutes later, I'm very happy with how I look. My hair is done up in a loose twist on the side of my head, letting the free hair fall over my shoulder. I check that my phone is still silent because I don't want anything to mess up this date.

This date is the one that I have been dreaming of since I was at least in the sixth grade.

I step out of the bathroom, and he's in dress pants and a button-down shirt, an outfit I'm sure he planned for the rehearsal dinner as well.

"Wow. You look stunning," he says as his eyes rake down my body and the hungry look in his eyes is a turn on.

"You cleaned up really good," I say without thinking as I run my eyes over his strong body.

He smiles before looking down at his feet and shoving his hands into his pockets.

He's nervous, and I can't remember the last time I saw him like this.

"I found a place on Route 66 I think you'll like," he says, holding out his hand for me.

When I take his hand, his smile matches mine. My hand fits perfectly in his as he leads me out to the car. He is a perfect gentleman and opens my door for me and everything.

On the way to the restaurant, we talk about what's on tomorrow's agenda for our drive. But when he pulls into Jack's Bar-B-Q, I think I fall for him even more, if that's possible.

"This place was on my list of want to eat at places!" I exclaim.

"I remember you talking about it, and when I saw it, I knew this is where we had to eat."

"It's perfect."

He gets out of the car and comes around to open my door, taking my hand in his as we enter. We get our food and take a seat. While we're a bit overdressed for this place, I don't care because it's perfect.

"I've had a crush on you since high school." He blurts out, shaking his head like he can't believe he just admitted that.

That somehow shocks me again, though I didn't think that was possible anymore today.

I place my hand over his.

"Well, I had a crush on you too."

***

Weston

I can't believe she liked me back then, too. All the things I'd have done differently if I had known run through my head.

Like asking her to be my date to prom or homecoming, and I might have even told her brother to shove it and take a chance with her.

But we were such different people back then. We both went off to school, and it probably wouldn't have worked out. Though I have compared every girl I've dated to her.

I need to change the subject because it's our first date and I don't want things to get too serious. Though it isn't like any normal first date, I know almost everything about her and have known her for years.

"So, how is Kinsley doing?" I ask her.

"Oh, she's fine. I guess there is some drama with her sister's boss, and her sister is trying to get her to fill in, so her sister can go interview with a new company."

"A twin switch? They haven't done that since they were in middle school."

"Yeah, remember when they tried to go to that party instead of studying? One studied for history, and one studied for math so they could take the same test twice. Then they changed clothes in the bathroom. It was a good plan. Too bad they got caught."

"What they didn't count on was the teachers being able to tell their handwriting apart," I laugh.

We finish our dinner and talk about things that happened in school, and I see all those memories with new eyes. Ones that know she liked me, making everything seem different.

Every look, every time she tagged along with me and her brother, every hug.

"Want to walk some of the shops in the outlet mall we passed on the way here?"

"Yeah, that sounds good."

It doesn't take long to get to the mall, and I know we really aren't here to shop. It's more of an excuse not to end the date and spend some more time together because things change once we head back to the hotel room.

She lets me hold her hand as we walk in and out of the shops browsing and enjoying the cool night.

On the way back to the hotel, the conversation flows, and she is smiling until we pull into the hotel parking lot. The mood shifts and even I feel slightly nervous.

Things are different now, which means a new dynamic once we get back to our room. I hadn't thought this far ahead.

She holds my hand as we walk to our door, but we don't say a word. Instead, I stop outside the door and look at her. Her pink lips are calling to me and I want to taste them again. Was it really only this morning I got my first taste of them?

Almost like she can read my mind, she licks her lips, and my eyes follow the movement of her tongue, and it pulls me in like a magnet. I hesitate just a centimeter away from her lips, giving her time to understand what's going to happen and to pull away. When she doesn't, I lean in and seal my lips to hers.

It's like coming home and it just feels right. Her lips are soft and taste like the lemonade she had with dinner. Pressing her against the door, I deepen the kiss. She wraps her arms around my waist and leans into me. Her little moans are making my cock hard, and I don't even try to hide it. What would she sound like underneath me if she let out these sexy moans from only a kiss?

I pin her to the door with my hips, and there is no doubt she feels how hard I am. She gasps, and I use this moment to tangle her tongue with mine.

Damn, she's a good kisser, and I've never had a kiss like this in my life. The elevator dings signaling that someone else is getting off on our floor. Reluctantly, I pull back from the kiss and put some space between us.

Pulling the key card out, I open the door for her and follow her into the room. She turns and opens her mouth to talk, but I need a moment to recover from that kiss.

"Go get ready for bed. We can talk more before bed."

She hesitates for only a moment before getting her stuff and going into the bathroom. I flop down on my bed and toss my arm over my face, so many thoughts running through my mind at once.

For one thing, I have to talk to her brother because he needs to hear this from me. Though I won't be shocked if he takes a swing at me for it. We still have over a week left on our trip and then a week of festivities before the wedding.

A week alone with her sounds like heaven, but a week separated from her when we reach California sounds like hell.

As the water shuts off, I get up and get my things together to take a shower. Then her phone goes off, and I find it sitting on her bed. It's her dad, so I pick it up and knock on the bathroom door.

"Your dad is calling." She opens the door and takes the phone from me and answers it as she gathers up her stuff.

"Your turn." She smiles at me, and I make a dash to the shower.

I'm still hard from that kiss, and even the cold shower isn't helping. The thought of jerking off crosses my mind for a brief moment, but I can't do that with her on the other side of the wall. Besides, I know it won't help anyway with the real thing nearby.

I guess this will be my permanent state for the rest of the trip.

By the time I get dressed and go back out to the room, she's off the phone.

"Everything all right?" I ask her.

"Yeah, dad was checking in and wanted to know what we saw so far. I think he's trying to follow us on a map."

She gets under the covers and lies on the edge of her bed facing mine, and I do the same. There is enough light coming in the window from the parking lot that I can still see her face.

"How will this work with my brother?" She asks the question we have been dancing around all night.

"He wants us to be happy, but you let me deal with him. I promise he will understand, though maybe just not right away," I answer.

I hope I'm right because my gut is not so sure.

Chapter 4

Rory

We got into Amarillo, Texas last night and are spending all day here. Apparently, one of Weston's friends from college is a cop just south of here and is coming up to meet us for dinner.

Things haven't changed much between West and me. We still have fun on the road, but we kiss more, and each night he takes me out to dinner. The days on the road we spend talking and getting to know each other in a new way and not just via the connection we have with Nate.

"So, what is on the list for today?" West asks as we go out to his car.

"First stop, we need to buy some spray paint."

"What the hell for?" He looks at me like I just sprouted a second head, and I can't help but laugh.

"For Cadillac Ranch!"

Since he is still looking at me like I'm weird, obviously, he doesn't know what Cadillac Ranch is.

"You know Cadillac Ranch? The place where some artist guy stuck ten classic Cadillacs in the dirt ass end up and now everyone stops, and spray paints a message or design to leave a piece of them on Route 66?"

"I know what it is, but it's the thought of you with spray paint that has me worried." He smirks as he pulls into a hardware store.

I fake gasp and playfully hit his arm. He rubs it, acting like the Hulk just sucker punched him.

Otherwise, he's a good sport, and together we pick up a few colors of spray paint and then head out to the ranch.

Luckily, there is only one family here, and they are down on one side, so we go over to the other.

"What are you going to paint?" I ask him.

"It's a secret." He gives me that sexy smirk like he knows it turns me on, and he's doing it on purpose.

We pick one of the cars at the end of the row, and he paints on the underbelly, and I start my design on the roof of the car. I figure I'll do something silly but cute in memory of us being here together.

So, with my lack of artistic skills, I spray paint a large heart and put both mine and West's initials in it.

"Ready when you are," I call out.

"Perfect timing! I'm ready too."

I join him on his side and gasp. He took my idea further and did it up like he was carving it into a tree trunk.

Rory + Weston = 4Ever

"It's perfect!" I giggle and snap a photo before moving over to his side.

"Looks like we were on the same wavelength." He wraps an arm around my shoulder and pulls me in for a hug, and kisses the top of my head.

"I think we need to do a Nate friendly one and send him a picture of it," I say, thinking out loud.

So, we head to the next car and write their wedding hashtag across it and then take a selfie photo together with it in the background and send it to both Nate and Mandy.

Then we grab a quick lunch before spending the rest of the afternoon at the RV museum. It was great to see some famous RVs from the movies and tour many of the models that you just know made their way down Route 66 at some time or another in history.

"When I have kids, I want to do summer road trips in an RV with them. Get out and see the country and spend time together over summer break." I say as we leave the museum.

"That sounds like a great idea. You ready for dinner?"

"Yeah, am I dressed okay, or should we stop and change?"

"You are dressed perfectly." His eyes run up and down my body appreciatively. My body breaks out in goosebumps as if he was actually touching me.

He clears his throat, "Ben picked out some fried chicken place. Everything is deep-fried and served in a basket. Nothing fancy."

On the drive there, I ask him about Ben.

"So, you two went to college together?"

"Yeah, he lives in a small town outside Amarillo, and he couldn't wait to go away to school, experience the world, and I guess we bonded over it. We were roommates freshman year and became fast friends and stayed roommates all through college. By the time we graduated, he couldn't wait to head home and settle in that small town."

"Does he know about us? Or is it okay if he does?"

"He knows how I felt, well feel, about you. I spilled my guts one night with a bit too much to drink after a bad date. It's why he was so willing to drive into Amarillo. He wants to meet you. We can tell him because he doesn't know Nate."

I nod as we pull into a place that has more outdoor picnic bench seating than seats indoors.

"West!" A man calls as we get out of the car.

"Ben. Good to see you."

"So, this is the famous Rory?" Ben walks over with his arms open to give me a hug, but West steps in front of him, stopping him.

"Don't touch," West growls, and Ben bursts out laughing.

"Let's go get some food. Think we have a lot to catch up on."

After we get our food, we snag a table outside in the shade, kind of away from everyone. Like a true cop, Ben takes the seat with his back toward the wall facing out so he can watch everything.

"So, did he finally admit his feelings for you?" Ben goes straight to the point.

"Yep, and I admitted my feelings for him."

"See! I told you she liked you! You should have made a move back then, man," Ben says.

Weston just shakes his head but smiles and changes the topic.

"First of all, no one can know. When we see her brother in a week, we'll tell him then. Second, are you seeing anyone?"

"I got it. And no. I just bought a small ranch at an auction, and when I'm not on duty, I'm busting my ass to get that place up and going. The house needs some love, and I should be able to move in next month. The land needs a lot more love, but a guy I went to high school with offered to help me out for just room and board."

"That great man! I know you were always torn between ranching and being a cop. Now you can do both."

"Yep, and eventually, I'll want to do one more than the other, and then I'll know for sure."

As we eat, they talk about old times and guys they knew in school.

"Where do you live, Ben?" I ask during one of the breaks in the conversation.

"Walker Lake, Texas. It's a beautiful, small town situated around Walker Lake. Many ranchers have lakes homes there for the few times they can get away."

During the conversation, West rests his hand on my leg, and suddenly that's all I can think about. I don't hear what they're talking about or notice anything happening around me.

My entire body is focused on West's hand on my bare thigh as he slowly rubs up and down my inner thigh. He ever so slowly moves a bit higher on each stroke. How is he paying perfect attention to Ben while he is driving me crazy like this?

When dinner is over, Ben says goodbye and goes out to his truck. But it takes me a bit longer to move because I can't take my eyes off of West as he clears our table off.

As we walk back to the car, he pulls me against his side, and his thumb slips under the bottom of my shirt. When he strokes the bare skin just above the top of my shorts, it once again drives me crazy.

The moment we get to the car he moves fast, and his lips are on mine, and he has me pinned to the side of the car. With his hips pushed into me, there is no mistaking how hard he is.

I wrap my arms around his neck and grind my hips against his hard cock, and he lets out a strangled groan and pulls back.

"Not here where anyone can see you. Tonight," he promises.

Tonight.

***

Weston

The drive back to the hotel is hell on my cock. Having her so close to me, but needing to concentrate on driving, didn't make things any easier. I can't seem to keep my hands off her, and the fact that she insists on wearing these short jean shorts everywhere doesn't help.

Being able to touch the soft skin of her inner thigh and see the goosebumps my touch causes is enough to drive any sane man crazy. My cock is so hard, I'm sure it's leaked enough pre cum to have a nice wet spot on the front of my jeans, and I don't even care.

When I stop at a red light, I don't expect her to lean over the center console and grip my cock.

"Fuck." I groan, throwing my head back against the headrest.

She starts stroking me over my jeans, and I just concentrate on not blowing my load like an over-excited teenage boy. Though I don't even realize my eyes are closed until the car behind us honks its horn because the light has turned green.

With a giggle, she removes her hand and settles herself back in her seat.

"Troublemaker," I whisper and place my hand back on her thigh, higher this time, and slowly trace the edge of the shorts until we pull into the hotel parking lot.

The moment I park, I'm out of the car and opening her door. Then I pin her to the car with a punishing kiss that I break before she's able to get her arms around my neck.

Taking her hand, I pull her behind me into the hotel. Thankfully, our room is on the ground floor.

"Hey, slow down. Not all of us are giants, you know," Rory says.

When I look back at her, she's practically running to keep up with me, so I slow my steps to allow her to catch up. Reaching our room, I open the door and pull us through and then pin her to it.

I waste no time getting my lips back on hers, but when she wraps her legs around my hips, I'm done for. Grinding into her, the moans tell me she is in as desperate need of release as I am. Increasing the pressure, I push into her again, intent on giving it to her.

"West," she gasps. "Wait! I want to taste you, please."

"Fuck." I want nothing more than to see her lips wrapped around my cock.

I grip her ass and carry her to the bed.

"You will always come first. That's non-negotiable with me. Can I taste you, baby girl?" I ask as I lay her down on the bed.

She nods her head, and I fall to my knees, pulling her ass to the edge of the bed. Slowly I unbutton her shorts sliding them down her long tan legs, revealing her light pink thong, which is soaked.

I groan, but before we pass the point of no return, I want her to know this isn't going any further, at least not tonight.

"This is all we're doing tonight. You understand?" I ask.

"Okay, just stop teasing me." Then she reaches for her panties and slowly pulls them down.

Swatting her hands away, I pull them down her legs myself. Then I run my hands back up the inside of her thighs, pushing them wide.

"You are so damn beautiful. I can't keep my hands off of you," I murmur. Not waiting any longer, I lean in and get my first taste of her.

I swear she tastes like berries and forever. How is that even possible?

Running my tongue over her clit, I pay special attention to her every movement and love the way her body moves against me. When she reaches out and grips my hair, I welcome the sting, knowing she is lost in the pleasure I'm giving her. There is no better compliment.

The harder she pulls my hair, the more aggressive I get. One moment she's moaning, and the next, her thighs clamp around my head in a death grip, and her body locks up as she cums all over my face. I lap up her cream, not wanting to waste a single drop, and resist the urge to hump the bed for just an ounce of relief.

When her body relaxes and goes limp, I finally look up at her, and she has a dreamy smile on her face, and her cheeks are flushed. Somehow, I get impossibly harder knowing I put that look on her face.

If I could, I'd stare at her like this all day. After a few minutes, she sits up then and pulls me in for a kiss which is sexy as hell.

"Your turn." She moves, and I barely get to my feet before she's unbuttoning my pants.

My back is against the wall, and I have a feeling I'm going to need the extra support because Rory is already on her knees in front of me. It's almost too much to take.

"I don't like the idea of you on your knees for anyone, even me," I tell her as I push some hair out of her face.

"Only for you." She smirks and pulls my pants and boxer down in one motion. My cock springs free and points right at her. He knows what he wants, and he isn't afraid to ask for it.

Rory wraps her hand around me and gives me a few hard pumps that make me lose my mind. Then she leans in and takes half my cock in one motion.

"Fuck!" I pound a fist into the wall behind me.

This is going to be over embarrassingly quick. I close my eyes and try to think of anything else, like the gory horror movie I watched last month. But when she cups my balls in her other hand, I jerk, not expecting it.

That's when I look down and see her pink lips stretched around my cock and her eyes looking up at me. It's a sight that I always want to remember. It's better than anything I ever imagined growing up when I'd picture this exact moment.

"I'm going to... " My warning is choked off when she sucks me in deep, and I started releasing rips of cum down her throat.

The sensation of her swallowing each one is almost more than I can take. I swear it feels like this orgasm is never-ending. Thank God for the wall behind me as I lock my knees, praying I can at least stay upright as my vision blurs.

The moment she slides my cock out of her mouth, I waste no time picking her up and taking her back to the bed. I pull my boxers up and leave my jeans on the floor and pull her in to cuddle.

"That was so perfect," I whisper and kiss the top of her head.

Only she doesn't get a chance to respond before her phone starts ringing.

Chapter 5

Rory

There is nothing like your semi-stalker best friend calling you right after a mind-blowing orgasm to put the brakes on everything. Kinsley called last night, and I didn't pick up. Instead, I texted her and told her I'd call her in a few days with an update. She wasn't happy but agreed.

Then West and I lay in bed cuddling and talking all night. I don't remember falling asleep, but I woke up to him kissing my neck. Waking up with him is another teenage fantasy come true.

Today we are driving into Albuquerque, New Mexico. West has been holding my hand in the car and has had a huge smile on his face all day. The weather has been beautiful. So we have the windows down and are enjoying it.

As we get closer to Albuquerque, the traffic slows down.

"I wonder what's going on." I pull up my traffic app, thinking there might be an accident on the road. We have been lucky so far and haven't hit much traffic.

"Oh! I don't know why I didn't check. The Balloon Fiesta is going on. Shoot, I would have loved to see it." I pout. Thinking it was next month, I didn't even bother to check.

"Why don't you try to find us a room, and we can stay and check it out tomorrow," he says.

"People book places a year in advance, so I doubt we will get anything."

"Call and ask if there were any cancellations and check with the vacation rentals."

"Those will be so much more expensive than a hotel!"

"It's on me. I think it would be kind of cool to see the balloons," West shrugs.

So, I get on the phone, and the third vacation rental place I call had a cancellation. The lady puts me on hold to pull up the details.

"She had a cancellation and is checking on it now," I whisper to West, letting myself get excited.

"Are you are there, dear?" the woman on the other line asks.

"Yes, I'm here."

"Okay, this is a three-bedroom condo, top floor, and you can watch the night show of the balloons from the balcony. It's always booked, so you are incredibly lucky. It normally books for three thousand a night this time of year, but due to the last minute cancellation I can let you take it for one thousand a night."

"Holy shit, that's expensive," I say as my heart sinks.

"Rory, I said I'd pay for it." West scolds me.

"But it's a thousand a night. Granted, we can watch the night show from the balcony, but still!"

"Book it, Rory." He pulls out his wallet and hands it to me.

"West..."

"Rory, book it for tonight and tomorrow night. We're crossing this off your bucket list, too," he says.

My eyes mist over at this wonderful gesture. Then I take his wallet and lean over, placing a kiss on his cheek before getting back to the woman on the phone. Booking the condo, I scribble down the address and check in instructions she gives me.

An hour later, we are stepping into the condo. It has a clean, modern design done in black and white. It's too big for just the two of us, but the view is fabulous. You can't beat it.

"Look, you can see some of the balloons from here!" It's all I can do not to jump and down like a kid.

"I got us tickets to the fiesta as well. I know a guy who owed me a favor." He comes up behind me, wrapping his arms around my waist as we look out the window.

"So, I'm thinking dinner, and then we can watch the night balloons take off right here on the balcony," West says.

"Sounds perfect."

***

Last night was amazing. We curled up on the balcony under a blanket with me on West's lap and watched the balloons light up the sky. I even video called Kinsley and showed her.

I sent a video to my brother, Mom, and Dad, who were all shocked we got this place last minute, much less tickets to the Balloon Fiesta.

Today we showed up early and plan to spend the whole day at the Balloon Fiesta. The guys setting up the balloons are more than happy to answer questions, and before long, the sky is filled with bright colors.

We watch balloon after balloon take off, and West pulls my back to his chest and wraps his arms around my waist, holding me close. Watching the balloons in the sky, me in West's arms, I can't remember the last time I was this happy or felt this safe.

Every so often, West looks down at me and places a soft kiss on my lips or forehead before looking at the balloons again. As the balloons get farther away, he looks at me, and this time our eyes lock and neither of us moves for a long moment.

Turning in his arms to face him, I put my arms around his waist, holding him close. He tucks a piece of hair behind my ear, something I notice he likes to do right before he kisses me. Only this time, he doesn't move closer, but he continues to stare into my eyes.

"I love you, Rory." His warm brown eyes never leaving mine.

My heart races. How long have I wanted to hear those words? How many nights did I stay up dreaming about them, imagining he was mine? Now the moment is here, and it's so much better than my teenage fantasy. Everything about this man is better than I could ever have imagined.

"I love you too, West, and think I have for a long time."

One of his blinding smiles lights up his face, making my heart skip a beat. Then he leans down and kisses me with an unbridled passion that leaves me breathless.

"Let's head back to the condo and I'll show you how much I love you," he whispers next to my ear. His warm breath brushes my ear and sends shivers down my spine.

"Okay." Is all I get out before he picks me up, throws me over his shoulder, and carries me back to the car like a caveman.

What have I gotten myself into?

***

Weston

All I can think about now is getting back to the condo. I'm in shock. She loves me too. I didn't mean to say the words out loud, but the more I looked into her eyes, the harder it became not to say anything.

Watching her enjoy the balloons and checking this off her bucket list hit me right in the heart. The look in her eyes matched how I felt, and I can't describe it, but to say it was breathtaking. But I knew without a doubt that this wasn't some teenage fantasy I was acting out, or a vacation fling, or like anything I had ever felt before.

At that moment, I couldn't imagine a life without her. Finally, the life I had wanted all this time seems in my grasp, and I want it.

Though the words tumbled out of my mouth uncontrollably, I couldn't have stopped them if I tried.

The last thing I expected was for her to say them back. For this beautiful, perfect woman to love me... *Me.*

I still can't believe it.

My one desire right now is to get us back to the condo quickly. The traffic in the area due to the balloons taking off is insane, and the throb in my cock only gets worse with each passing moment. Her scent fills the car, and a single thought runs through my mind... *she's mine.*

Once again, the moment we get in the condo, I pin her with her back to the door. I find myself doing this a lot with her. Maybe it's something about not being able to wait to get my hands and lips on her. Or it's about crowding her, so her attention is on me and only me.

When my lips meet hers, it's like my body can finally relax. She's mine, she's home, and she's not going anywhere. Though my cock does the opposite of relaxing. It knows what it wants, her and only her.

"Say it again," I growl.

"I love you, West."

"I love you too, baby girl. So damn much."

My lips are on hers again. As much as I want to take her to bed and make love to her, I want to remember this moment, this kiss, and this surrender to each other. She's mine, and I'm hers and this point in time seals the deal.

"No going back. You are mine."

"That's all I ever wanted, West." She wraps her legs around my waist and her arms around my neck.

My hands go to her firm ass, sliding as far as I can under her shorts, kneading the baby soft flesh. Turning, I carry her to the bedroom, where I don't plan to let her leave until we absolutely have to tomorrow.

I lay her on the bed and remove her clothes like I'm unwrapping a present. Once she's naked and lying on the bed, I want her even more. She looks like an angel against the white sheets. Keeping my eyes riveted on her, I remove my clothes while her eyes caress me as she makes her way down, landing on my cock.

She wants this as bad as I do, which spurs me on to make this especially good for her. I have to, there is no choice.

I fall to my knees between her thighs and spread her legs wide. Though I want to go slow and make this last all night, I'm so hard and turned on that taking my time isn't going to happen.

"Next time, baby girl, I'll go slowly. I just need you too bad right now," I promise her. Then I do what I've wanted to all day. I suck her clit into my mouth and swirl my tongue around it before letting my tongue explore lower.

"I don't want slowly. I want you now." She tries to pull me up to her. I give her clit a little more attention before I move up her body, ghosting my lips over the skin of her stomach.

When I get to her breasts, I give them some needed attention, nipping and sucking on them before moving further up to her neck, then to her mouth as I settle over her. I keep my weight off but still pin her to the bed. She reciprocates by wrapping her legs around my waist, her arms tight around my neck, wiggling closer.

I pull back, but she doesn't want to let me go. Breaking her hold, I tell her I need to get a condom and walk over to my bag.

Grabbing a condom from the box I picked up at a stop a few days ago, I roll it on. When I walk back over to her and settle in the same spot, she wastes no time wrapping her arms and legs around me again.

This time when she lifts her hip, I nudge my cock to her slick entrance. The feeling of her warmth on my tip sends me into sensory over-load. We're at the moment I've been wanting. It doesn't feel real, and the teenage boy I was all those years ago never had an imagination this good.

Resting my weight on my arms, I frame her face with my hands and kiss her as I slowly slide into heaven. The only one I will ever enter again. I know in the depth of my soul, at this moment, this girl will always be mine.

The further I slide into her, the tighter her grip on me gets, making it harder for me to fill her completely. But the feel of her tight and wet around my cock is enough to make me come on the spot if I'm not careful.

"Relax, baby girl, let me in," I whisper against her lips as I place soft kisses all over her face.

All I get in response is a moan as she tries to find my lips again. I make slow, shallow thrusts until I'm all the way inside her, then I pause and soak in this moment in time.

She is running her hands through my hair, and her legs are digging into my hips, and life is perfect.

"I love you, baby girl," I tell her because I can't seem to keep it in now that I've said it.

"I love you too, West," she groans as I start thrusting again.

Her pussy flutters around me, and I know she's as close as I am. As much as I want to drag our first time out and make it last for hours, the need to make her cum is stronger.

I reach down and put pressure on her clit, and on my next thrust her body locks up around mine, and she comes with a silent scream. Her pussy is a vice around my cock, and I couldn't stop myself from coming if my life depended on it.

Finally, I pull out only long enough to get cleaned up and rejoin her in bed.

Having her curled up to me skin on skin is addicting. Her warm body, soft skin, and feminine curves are heaven against my body. I don't think I want clothes between us ever again.

"What happens to us when we get home?" she asks.

"We date. I try to convince you to spend weekends at my place so I can spoil you. As long as we do it together, we go at whatever pace is comfortable for you."

I run my hand up and down the smooth skin on her back, thinking of all the dates I want to take her on. There is so much to do back in Chicago, so much to explore. All the things I want to experience with her, like taking a boat down the river, visiting the aquarium, Navy Pier, the museums, catching a concert at Millennium Park, and so much more.

"Well, I'll be looking forward to a few weekends at home snuggling on the couch and watching TV and being totally lazy after this," she says.

"I can get on board with that. Cuddling with you, I'm quickly finding, is my new addiction." I kiss the top of her head.

Because I can't seem to stop, I say, "I love you, baby girl.".

Her "I love you too," is music to my ears.

We lay there a while longer when my phone goes off. The caller ID says it's her brother, so I send it to voicemail. The last thing I want to do is talk to him while I have his sister naked and pressed against me with a post orgasm glow. I don't want him ruining this moment.

In the back of my mind, I know I have to talk to him. No matter how much I reassure Rory, I don't think he's going to take too kindly to us being together.

Chapter 6

Rory

I didn't want to leave the condo yesterday but West suggested we head into Flagstaff last night and get a room for a couple of nights in order to see the Grand Canyon while we're there, and I agreed. Really any extra time with him and I'm on board.

We stopped at Petrified Forest National Park, the iconic Wigwam Motel in Holbrook, Arizona, and took our picture 'Standin' on a Corner in Winslow Arizona' while we badly sang The Eagles song. Then we made a slight detour to a meteor crater site just off Route 66 before driving into Flagstaff last night.

Things have changed between us, and I'm loving every minute of us. Last night he still took me to dinner, but when we got home, he made love to me again and then held me all night.

Today we're heading to the Grand Canyon. Even though Flagstaff boasts you can stay there and visit the Grand Canyon, it's still an almost two-hour drive one way. But we're on a road trip, so we're used to this.

My new favorite way to sit while West drives is to turn in my seat and put my back to my door and my feet in his lap. He'll keep one hand on me at all times, rubbing my feet, or up my leg driving me crazy. I can feel how hard he gets, so I know it excites him, too. Every so often, he'll look over at me with a big smile lighting up his face, making both my heart happy and my pulse race.

It's definitely a more interesting road tripping with him than alone, and someday I'll thank my brother for this. Well, after he cools off, of course.

Once at the Grand Canyon, we decided to do the Skywalk that juts out over the edge of the canyon. It's made of glass so you can see the chasm below you and it is supposed to have great views.

"You sure you're up for this baby girl? I know you aren't a fan of heights..."

"I'm not, but this is one instance where I need to face my fear. I'm not missing out on this, plus I have you." I grab onto his arm.

"I won't let anything happen to you. You can count on that."

"Knowing that makes it a little easier to do."

Looking at pictures on the way here, I thought it would be easy to do, no problem. But now that I'm here and see how high up we are and how far this skywalk circles out, my nerves are in high gear.

"We can turn around any time, just say the word," West says, wrapping an arm around my waist.

"No way. We're taking a photo right there in the middle to send to Nate, so he leaves us both alone for a few days."

West is patient with me, even as I'm sure we get passed by a snail on our way out to the center. He never once complains or tries to rush me. Mostly, he offers support and tries to distract me.

When we reach the center, I just keep telling myself not to look down.

"Ok, let's snap this photo and then get back to solid ground," I say, and West pulls out his phone and stands next to me, getting a great shot of the canyon behind me. Then we turn and make sure to get the skywalk behind us.

"Now I want a photo for us," he stands behind me, pulling me close and wrapping an arm around my waist. My nerves ease slightly and when he kisses my neck, I almost forget where we are. We snap a few pictures, including one of us kissing before we leave the skywalk.

It goes without saying I moved much faster to get off the death trap than I did to get on it. When we get back to the car, West pulls me into his arms.

"I am so proud of you! You did great out there." Then leans down to kiss me.

"It took me, what an hour, to even make my way out there," I say, pulling back.

"No, only forty-five minutes. You did amazing. Now, do we want to spend more time here, or go down to Sedona and have dinner there?"

"Let's do Sedona, but first, let's send the photo to Nate."

We get in the car, and West first sends all the photos to me, then sends the first two to Nate. Who as expected, calls minutes later after receiving them."

"Hey man, you're on speakerphone. We are just leaving the Grand Canyon."

In reality, we're still sitting in the parking lot holding hands because we knew he'd call.

"Shit. I can't believe you got Rory out there on the ledge like that!" Nate says.

"Hello, I'm right here." I roll my eyes.

"Rory did great, took her time, but she did it, and we've got proof of it," West says.

"I didn't realize the Grand Canyon was on your stop list," Nate says.

"It wasn't. We stopped in Flagstaff and decided to visit since we kept seeing all the signs for it. More like I convinced Rory to go."

"Damn guys, you keep adding time, and you'll miss the wedding," Nate says.

"Oh, they will not," Mandy says in the background, and the sound of her playfully slapping my brother fills the line.

"We will be back on the road tomorrow," I tell him, trying to get his attention back.

"You guys having fun, though? I saw the photos of the Balloon Fiesta, and now Mandy is insisting we go next year."

"You should. It was well worth the stop," I say.

"The whole trip has been worth it. I'm glad you suckered me into it." West says while his eyes are on me, clearly having a double meaning to his words.

"Well, keep her safe and no more delays!" Nate says.

"No promises!" I say at the same time West says, "I will."

We hang up, and the moment the call ends West's lips on mine again.

***

Weston

We make the drive down to Flagstaff and then Arizona 89A into Sedona. Rory looked it up online, and it's supposed to be this beautiful scenic route where we get to see the Sedona red rocks up close.

"Can we go see the Chapel of The Holy Cross before dinner? It's the church built into the red rocks." Rory says, turning the radio down.

This is the first time she has spoken since the call with her brother.

"Of course, just put it in the GPS." I nod toward the dashboard.

After setting the GPS, she sits back and places her feet on the dashboard. She looks so damn sexy like that. But I can tell something is on her mind, and I don't want any secrets between us. I can't help her and support her if she doesn't open up to me.

"What's on your mind?" I reach over to take her hand in mine simply for the connection.

"What do we do when we get to the wedding?"

"What do you want to do?" I ask her because I know what I want.

I want to talk to her brother the moment we get there. Then I want her in my bed, in my arms everywhere so I can show her off.

"Well, I want to talk with my brother but..."

I was over the moon excited until I heard that but.

"But what?"

"This is their weekend and their event. I know Nate won't be happy, and I don't want to ruin it."

"I agree, so maybe I'll talk to him myself, but we keep us on the down low from everyone else. But I still want to spend as much time with you as I can."

"Ok, that works. I agree." She seems to loosen up at this and relax.

"You know," she says, "I was looking forward to this trip the moment my brother said he was getting married. I was even looking forward to the wedding. Now, not so much."

"Why not, baby girl?" I ask her.

"Because when we get there, everything will change. I know we will still be us, yet while we're in this car, on this trip, I feel like we are in a bubble where it's just you and me. When we get there, the bubble bursts, and we have to let everyone else in. I kind of like having you all to myself."

I squeeze her hand because I know exactly what she means.

"Well, I don't want this bubble to pop either, but we can get it back when we return to Chicago. Those lazy nights in front of the TV where I get to hold you for hours will be even better than this. You'll see."

She sighs and forces a smile, "I know you're right."

We visit the Chapel, get some photos and even get to peek inside. She walks down the aisle to the front of the church, where a huge glass wall looks out over the Sedona red rocks. The view is breathtaking, but the thoughts filling my head are even more so.

Visions of her walking down the aisle to me, all dressed in white, fill my head, and suddenly, I want it more than anything.

But we just started dating, and her brother doesn't even know about us. If I proposed to her now, I'd send her running for the hills. But I can't deny that the thought of us getting married doesn't scare me like the thoughts of marrying my ex did.

Maybe I always knew it was Rory, even if I don't think I ever had a shot in hell with her.

We head to downtown Sedona and grab dinner at a place with outdoor seating and the most beautiful views of the mountains surrounding the city.

While we're sitting side by side facing the mountains, watching the sunset behind us, she says, "I could sit here all day and just stare at the views."

Nodding, I agree with her. "I wish they had places like this back in Chicago."

"We have restaurants that overlook Lake Michigan and the Chicago River."

"True, but it's just not quite the same. The city is not as quiet, and it's a concert jungle instead of the nature feel here."

"Planning on leaving the city?" She bumps my shoulder.

"No, but it's good to get away every now and then and get back into nature,"

"I agree. Something about being here soothes the soul."

It's a bit of a drive back to our hotel after dinner, and while we talked earlier, I can tell thoughts are still running through her head.

"Come, take a shower with me," I say, tempting her.

Once under the warm water, I massage her shoulders, and she starts to relax and melt into me.

"Ooh, that feels so good."

"You're stressing about all this with your brother. I can tell it's on your mind. You just let me handle it, okay? I promise I'll talk to him and take care of this."

"But he's still my brother. And I can't help feeling like this will blow up in our faces. I just know it."

"But he wants you to be happy. He always has, and always will."

"I know."

Turning her to face me, I grab the soap and start slowly washing her, beginning at her shoulders and slowly moving over her breasts and down her hips. Then I sink to my knees, washing her legs and feet.

I know one sure way to make her relax and plan to use it. Then I lift one of her legs over my shoulder and lean in to suck on her clit.

"West!" she gasps, reaching out to grip the shower wall.

I keep playing with her clit, then thrust my tongue into her and feast on her cream. She is already so wet, and if she was half as turned on today as I was, I know she needs a release, and I'm just the man to give it to her.

Relentlessly, I stroke her clit with my thumb as I lap at her pussy. Faster than I expected, she goes off like a rocket. Her legs start to shake, and I reach up and hold her steady as she soaks my face, moaning my name.

After her breathing quiets and she slumps against me, I hold her for a minute before I say, "Now let's wash up so I can take you to bed and make love to you all night."

Chapter 7

Rory

Leaving Flagstaff is bittersweet. We cross into California today, and it's like a big bucket of cold water to remind us that this bubble is ending soon. Despite that, we still plan to enjoy the rest of the trip. So, like always on travel days, the music is cranked up, the windows are down, West in driving, my feet are in his lap, and his hand is in mine.

When we are driving around back home, I hope this doesn't stop. His hand on my thigh or in my hand, while he drives, is sexy as hell, and I don't ever want him to quit.

We stop and get lunch at a classic Route 66 diner, and as much as I love all the diner food, I'm sure I've put on ten pounds by now. Though with all the crazy hot sex with West, I'm just as sure I'm well on my way to burning it off.

"So," I ask West, "how do you feel about making tomorrow a shorter day? There is another Wigwam Motel in San Bernardino, and they have a vacancy. I think it would be cool to stay there for a night."

"Let's do it. The ones in Holbrook, Arizona, were really cool looking."

I glance over at him. "Nate will have something to say about another delay."

Whenever I bring up my brother, I always feel weird. West says not to be anxious, and he'll handle it, but I do worry.

We get into Needles, California, and get a room. Then we head out to explore a bunch of the old Route 66 motels and gas stations. We take our photo in front of the famous Welcome to Needles Railroad Borax Wagon.

I send that photo to Nate.

Me: Look, we are in the same state now!
Nate: Finally! Are you having fun?
Me: Yeah. Honestly, it's been nice having West here and not having to drive the whole thing. I took so many photos.
Nate: I can't wait to hear all about it. When you get here, I have lunch set aside, just you and me to catch up.
Me: Can't wait.

While I do want to catch up with my brother, the thought of having lunch with him makes my stomach do flip flops. If he knows, I'm sure that's all he will harp on, and if he doesn't, I'll feel nothing but guilt keeping it from him. Really, this is a no-win situation.

"So, I'm thinking we grab dinner and take it back to our room tonight," West says pulling me from my thoughts. "There is a storm rolling in, and maybe we can just relax and watch some TV?"

"Sounds perfect. What are you in the mood for?"

"There is a retro diner up the road there. Want to go see what they have?"

"Sounds good," I agree.

Thirty minutes later, we are back in our room with dinner spread out picnic-style on the bed as we try to decide what to watch.

"How about one chick flick and one action movie?" he says, referring to the romantic comedies I like to watch.

"I agree so long as it's not too gory."

"I know you don't like blood and guts, so I promise to pick a mild one."

We clean up and settle in to watch TV. I'm in his arms, my back to his chest, and not even ten minutes into the movie his hand starts wandering, and he's kissing the back of my neck. I turn to kiss him, but he stops me.

"Watch the movie, baby girl. I know you like this one."

I nod and try to concentrate on the TV, but when his hand unbuttons my shorts and dips below my panties, there is nothing in the world that would pull my attention from what's going on down there. Slowly he moves one hand and palms my breasts over my shirt, and then with the other, he strums my clit.

Not able to sit still, I rub my ass against his hard cock, and he groans, removing his hand.

"Watch the movie," he whispers in my ear again as he pulls my leg up and back over his hip.

I try to focus on the movie, but then his hand slides down my tummy towards my aching core. I can't breathe, just waiting for his hand to soothe my ache. When his finger slides and rolls over my clit, I gasp, ready for more.

Does he really think I can concentrate on the TV with the things he's doing to my body right now?

He begins thrusting into me as his thumb plays with my clit. But it's all lazy movements like he plans to drag it out like we have all night because we do.

"How are you watching TV with your eyes closed?" he whispers into my ear.

I didn't even realize my eyes were closed. Opening them, I try to focus on the moving colors in front of me, but nothing on TV makes sense when my body is on fire. He's keeping me on the edge of the orgasm my body has been craving all day.

"West, please," I moan.

Finally, he picks up the pace and increases the pressure on my clit while he nips at my earlobe and neck. My body is on sensory overload and every nerve tingles as I scream out his name and cum all over his fingers. But he doesn't slow down, dragging out my orgasm until I'm pretty sure I'm nothing but a big bowl of Jell-O.

Only then does he pull his fingers from me and bring them to his mouth to suck clean before wrapping me in a huge bear hug.

He buries his face in my hair and groans. "How am I supposed to go back to sleeping without you in just a few days?"

"It's just a few days. Think of it as an incentive to talk to my brother. The sooner you get it out of the way, the sooner I'll be back in your bed."

"If you aren't in mine, I'll be in yours, don't ever doubt it. I'll find a way," he says.

I don't doubt he will.

***

Weston

Never thought I'd enjoy a road trip this much. But when I'm driving, and Rory places her feet in my lap, and she relaxes next to me, I don't want the car ride to end.

When she sees so many of the classic Route 66 stops that she's only read about, I love watching her face light up. Even taking all the photos with her at almost every stop is something I've grown to love. Even though I get to be part of the memories she'll always have of this bucket list trip, this is just the beginning for us. I have plans for when we get home.

We pull into the Wigwam Motel in San Bernardino, California, and I'm glad we decided to stop here. The motel has been kept up with many of the original details. You can see the mountains in the distance, and it's a bonus that they have a pool.

Our room has a queen bed, a small sitting area with a leather couch, a TV, and a bathroom. All in all, it's a nice room for a tent-shaped room.

"Let's go grab some food, then I plan to spend the rest of the night with you in this room." After we drop off our bags, I take her hand and head back to the car.

There is a taco place right down the road, so we grab tacos and talk about anything and everything that isn't Nate and the wedding.

"Kinsley has been hounding me about details on what is going on with me and you." She says as her phone goes off for the third time since we sat down to eat.

"What did you tell her?"

She can tell Kinsley anything she wants, as long as it includes that she's mine. If she wants, she can share every detail. Because I know they're close, and I won't ever stop her from sharing with her friend. We all need someone to talk to.

"I promised her a girl's night when we get home, and I'd tell her everything and answer all her questions, but she is impatient."

"If you want to call her, go ahead."

"No, I want to spend time with you while I can. I'll touch base with her in a few days when we get to..." she shrugs.

When we get to Napa for the wedding. She's quiet as she eats, and I want to get us back to a good place and push away this dark cloud because I don't like the squeezing of my heart at the thought of having to pretend this girl isn't mine.

"So tomorrow we hit the Santa Monica Pier. Whatever we do, we have to get pictures at the famous end of the trail sign."

"Yes, for sure. I can't believe as of tomorrow, we will have driven all of Route 66. This has been my dream for so long that it doesn't seem real now that I'm finally completing it."

"I always knew you would. You wanted it too much not to do it. What will your next bucket list item be?"

"I've been thinking about the trip, and after visiting the Ground Canyon, I think I want to visit every National Park in the United States. There are sixty-three National Parks if you include The Grand Canyon. Now I've been to eight of them. I think it's a good goal, and it will help me travel more and experience more nature."

"That's a good goal. We could head out to Montana and do Glacier, Yellowstone, and Grand Tetons this summer," I say without thinking.

Her eyes go wide before she looks down at her plate. I just made plans for roughly seven months from now and tipped my hand. Well, I'm in this for the long haul, and the sooner she realizes that, the better.

We finish up our meal in comfortable silence before going back to the motel. Once in our room, I sit on the couch and pull her onto my lap.

"What I said back there, I meant it, baby girl. I am in this for the long haul." I try to clear the air.

"I want what you do, but I'd be lying if I said I wasn't worried about telling Nate about us and how it will affect us. Everything changes when we get there. When people start finding out about us, they'll have their own opinions."

To stop her thoughts and her rambling, I lean in and kiss her. I get where she is coming from. We got together during an escape from life, and real everyday life will be different. But I have no doubt that it will be even better.

With this kiss, I try to convey all of our wants and desires. I want her to trust in me, to let me shoulder the weight of this. Then I carry her to the bed, and our lovemaking is more desperate because change is in the air, and we both know it.

***

"I can't believe it's over," Rory says as we stand in front of the Route 66 end of the trail sign.

Both of us stare at it in almost disbelief. It's the end of the road trip, the marker that says Rory can check Route 66 off her bucket list, and yet I feel jipped. The trip went by too fast, and I want a do-over. I want more time.

"Come on, let's get our photo, then I want to ride the Ferris wheel with you." We take our just friends photo that will get sent to her brother and parents. Then we take our couples photos with her in my arms and us kissing in front of the sign.

She sends the photos to her brother, who turns around and calls almost immediately.

We walk to a quiet place out of the way, and she puts him on speakerphone.

"You did it! How does it feel?" Nate asks.

"Yup, I finally did it. But it went by too fast, and it was better than I expected." Her eyes meet mine when she says that, and I couldn't agree more. I kiss her forehead because I don't think pulling her in for a passionate kiss with her brother on the phone is a good idea.

"So, you'll be here in what a day or two?" Nate asks.

"That's the plan. We're going to see the Santa Monica Pier tonight and head up to Napa first thing tomorrow. Depending on traffic," she says.

"Be careful and don't give West a hard time. You're almost free of him."

A pit forms in my stomach. I don't want her free of me, but I can't say that, and I can tell Rory isn't too happy that I can't speak up either.

"See you soon, brother," Rory tells him and ends the call.

"You will never be free of me, baby girl. Do you understand me? Never."

Chapter 8

Rory

We decide to drive the Pacific Coast Highway from Los Angeles to San Francisco for the views. We were also hoping to avoid any major traffic delays on the interstate. But it's like fate decides West and I deserved more time together because an hour into our trip, there is a major backup due to several car accidents.

After an hour in traffic, only to move about five miles, I text Nate.

Me: Been in traffic for an hour already.

I attach a photo of the backup.

Nate: Of course, you hit traffic when you are finally on your way here * eye roll emoji *
Me: It's a sign. I'm going to head home instead * laughing emoji *
Nate: Don't you dare.
Me: We will be there... eventually.

Nate: Be safe.

I have a very similar conversation with my parents before putting my phone down and turning to West.

"It's a sign, isn't it?"

"What is?" he asks, reaching over and taking my hand in his now that it's free again.

"This backed up traffic. It's delaying us because things are going to go horribly at the wedding. Not for Nate and Mandy, but for us."

He squeezes my hand. "You can't think like that. Positive thoughts only. See, the road is opening up."

Sure enough, as we round the next curve, we can see the accident, and just past it, traffic starts moving again. The drive is beautiful the rest of the day. After we stop for lunch and are on the road again, we begin seeing the signs for San Francisco telling us we're getting closer and closer. But my stomach sinks more and more.

Just on the other side of San Francisco is Napa Valley and the destination I've been dreading for a week now. Almost like West can sense my dread, he pulls off the highway in Carmel-by-the-Sea.

"What are you doing?" I ask as he pulls into a historic little hotel.

He turns to me. "One more night. I need one more night with you," he pleads in a tone that sounds as desperate as I feel.

When I nod in agreement, he's out of the car and checking us in before I even get a text off to my brother that we're stopping tonight due to traffic and will be there tomorrow. I put my phone on silent and join West as he leaves the reception desk with our keys.

Once In our room, he does my favorite thing after dropping our stuff to the floor. He pins me to the door in a kiss so hot and full of desire my pussy spasms. But he doesn't let the kiss go too far.

"I have to feed you. The hotel has a restaurant, and I thought we could watch the sunset on the beach. We can walk there from here."

"Sounds perfect." I try to pull him in for another kiss.

"If I kiss you again, we won't leave this room," he groans.

"I don't see a problem with that." I try to pull him down again.

"Don't get me wrong. I want you," he grinds his erection into me. "But this is more than sex for me. I want to watch the sunset on the beach in California with my girlfriend before we both get sucked into the chaos of my best friend's wedding."

My heart flutters, and I forget to breathe when he calls me his girlfriend. It's the first time he's done so, and for it to be here and for such a romantic reason, I couldn't think of better timing if I tried.

"That sounds like the perfect date."

And it is. At dinner, we talk, and we laugh and have a really great time with some good food. As we walk to the beach, hand in hand, we enjoy the last bit of freedom we'll have to touch each other freely. Though neither of us says it out loud.

Once we get to the sand, we take off our shoes, and since we're in shorts, we walk up to the water and sink our feet in. West stands behind me, wrapping his arms around my waist, holding me close as we watch the sunset and take in the sky painted in beautiful reds, oranges, and yellows as the waves crash over our feet.

It's a perfect moment that I wish would never end. The outside world can't touch me here in West's arms, and it's here I start to think we can weather any storm. So I begin to feel more confident about tomorrow. As long as West is at my side, I can face anything.

After we're back at the hotel, it's like all bets are off. We can't get our clothes off fast enough.

The sex isn't gentle. It isn't drawn out either. It's urgent and fast as if we need to claim each other and prove he's mine and I'm his. We don't even make it to the bed. He takes me right against the door, and I'm sure anyone walking down the hallway knew exactly what we were doing.

It was perfect and exactly what I needed to ease my tension. Too bad the pit in my stomach is still there.

***

Weston

Neither of us wants the trip to end. I'm driving slowly to Napa Valley and letting everyone pass by us. Rory hasn't complained once because I know she feels the same way.

Last night was what I'd consider a perfect night. Having dinner with her, watching the sunset with her in my arms on the beach with the sand between our toes and the water washing over our feet, was the very definition of romance. And something we'll always remember.

Then when we got back to our room, we made love all night.. I hope it made her understand how I feel about her.

We are an hour away from the vineyard where Nate and Mandy will have their wedding and all the events. Everyone is staying there, and it's supposed to be beautiful.

The bachelor and bachelorette parties are tonight, and I know we can't miss those. We are already three days later than we had planned, but I can't be sorry for that. It's three extra days I got my girl to myself.

When we're about twenty minutes away from the vineyard, we pass a rest stop on the highway just before our exit. Taking advantage of one last reprieve, I pull over and park in the back of the parking lot away from everyone else, and turn to face her.

"I hate this," I say, figuring it's best to be brutally honest.

"Me too, but you know we can't miss tonight, and we're out of excuses."

"I know." I move in for a kiss, desperate to taste her again because I know the moment we get there, we will be pulled in two different directions.

Our kiss turns desperate and passionate, and we make out like teenagers in the car, and I memorize everything. How she tastes, the little moans she makes, how her lips move with mine, and the feel of her hands in my hair.

She's wearing a skirt today, and she looks so damn beautiful. But I'm grateful for the skirt because when I run my hand up the inside of her thigh to her panties, I find them wet.

"You need me, baby girl?" I ask.

"Always, West. I always need you." She moans and tries to shift her hips to get my fingers where she wants them.

Does she know what her words do to me? They calm the beast in me who is clawing at his cage, knowing in half an hour I have to pretend like she isn't my whole world.

"I love you," I whisper against her lips.

"I love you too, West," she says, and only then do I move her panties to the side and start playing with her clit.

She is wet and needy, moving with my hand and trying to pull me closer. If we weren't in a public place, I'd lay my seat back, pull her over me and have her ride my dick until she orgasmed so many times she'd sleep right through the next few days.

But right now, I'll settle for making her come all over my hand and walking in to see her brother with her taste still on my tongue and her panties soaked from me.

Taking my time, I slowly start playing with her clit, driving her to the edge only to let up before she falls over. Then I thrust two fingers into her, curling them slightly and hitting the spot inside her that drives her crazy. When I know she is close again, I pull my fingers out, and she gives a frustrated moan.

I bury my head in her neck so she can't see my smile. Already, I know her body almost better than she does, and I can keep her on edge for hours if I want. Maybe one night, I'll tie her to my bed and do just that.

When I begin playing with her clit again, she tries to reach for my cock. But I grab her hands, pulling them behind her and holding both her wrists in one of my hands. This is about me claiming her, and I want her to enjoy every minute of it.

I go back to playing with her clit slowly, as slowly, and as lazily as I'm kissing her. She keeps trying to move her hips to grind against me, but with her arms behind her back, she can't move far. I slide two fingers into her again, easily and without increasing my pace, I thrust in and out of her.

"You're mine, Rory," I tell her, wanting to make myself clear.

"Yes," she moans.

"And I'm yours. The moment this wedding is over, no more hiding."

I won't cause a scene and ruin Nate's day, but I won't stay separated from her a moment longer than I have to.

"Okay." She agrees, and that's what I needed to hear.

I continue playing with her clit and stroking the magic spot inside her. Her pussy starts to flutter, and I swear I feel it on my cock. As she starts to cum, I pull back and watch the orgasm roll over her.

There is nothing sexier than watching my girl let go like this for me. The flush which creeps up her cheeks, the way her eyes roll back in her head, and her mouth falls open. These are memories that will get me through the next few nights. This is probably a memory I'll be reliving on my deathbed. Without a doubt, I know it.

When she relaxes into me, I pull my fingers from her and fix her panties before bringing my fingers to my mouth and sucking them clean. Her taste on my tongue is almost enough to make me come in my pants, but I keep it together.

She tries to reach for me when I let go of her wrists, but I stop her and gently bring her hand up to my mouth and place a kiss in the center of her palm.

"The next time I cum will be in you," I tell her, and her eyes go slightly wide before she pulls me down for a kiss.

"Let's get this wedding over with." She fixes herself and settles back into her seat.

"Yes, let's."

Chapter 9

Rory

As we pull into the winery, I can already tell it's going to be a madhouse. I reluctantly let go of West's hand and though he frowns, says nothing. The moment we stop at the front entrance, my mom, Mandy, and a few other bridesmaids are there, along with Nate and my dad.

I don't even get my seatbelt off before they're opening my car door, and I barely get both feet on the ground before Mom and Mandy are wrapping me in a hug.

"How was the trip?"

"Can I see the pictures?"

"Tell me everything!"

They rapid-fire at me so fast I'm not sure who says what.

A quick glance as West shows he's getting the second degree from Nate and my dad as well.

"I had the best time, and I'll show you photos later."

Yeah, like after I move the couples photos of West and me to a secure folder they can't get to.

"We have your room over on the girl's wing with us," Mom says.

"The guys are staying on the other side of the the winery so we can do girls' night and everything!" Mandy says.

That also means it will be that much harder for West and me to sneak around.

"Mom, you and Dad aren't sharing a room?" I ask.

"Nope, I needed some girl time, but we find ways to sneak around," she winks at me.

"Gross! Mom!" I cover my ears and turn away to find West watching me with a smirk on his face.

"Why don't you go with them? I'll bring you bags to your room," West says.

"Oh yes! Come on, I want to show you around. This place has everything." Mandy starts pulling me inside.

"You can't take her anywhere until I get to say hi to my little sister," Nate says, pulling me into a hug.

"Missed you," I say because, despite everything, I have missed him.

"Missed you too, and I told you having West on the trip wouldn't be that bad!"

"Yeah, you say that now, but boy, do I have stories to tell," I say with a wink and then let myself be pulled away by Mandy.

One last look over my shoulder, and I see West watching me go. Why does it feel so wrong to be walking away from him like this? We've been attached at the hip for just over two weeks, so that has to be it. It will be good to get a bit of space, healthy even, I try to tell myself.

"Ok, so there is a day spa down here and a salon where we're getting our hair done the day of the wedding." Mandy points them out just off the lobby.

I know she asked me to be a bridesmaid because I'm Nate's sister, and I was excited to do it. Now I realize it means less time being able to sneak around with West.

"Mandy, ask her now so we can start planning," Mom says.

My stomach sinks. This has to be big if they waited until I was here in person.

"So, my maid of honor decided to go learn how to surf. She took a nasty fall and broke her leg. I see now Nate wasn't joking that there is always drama at your family's weddings. My niece can be a junior bridesmaid, and we got her a dress, but will you fill in as maid of honor? Please, please, please say you'll do it," Mandy begs.

I look at my mom, who is standing just beside her. She has a smile on her face. Looking over to the side at the other bridesmaids, Mandy's friends, they all wear smiles too.

"Of course, I'll fill in. Let's get you married!" I say because really there is no way you can say no in a situation like this, even though I basically just signed away any free time I had left.

"Okay, so let's give you the grand tour," Mandy says.

She shows me the grounds where the wedding will be held, outside, including the cute little bridges she will be crossing as she walks down the aisle. The arch is being set up, and the backdrop of the grapevines and the mountains are picture perfect. She timed it perfectly as the leaves are starting to change colors and will make for some killer wedding photos.

We then head back inside, and she shows me the reception room, the bar, the restaurant, and where we will be getting ready downstairs before we go up to our rooms in our wing.

"So tonight will be kind of low-key. We are going to a wine bar in town, doing dinner, drinking wine, dancing, singing some karaoke. Just want to have fun. Nate hired a car for us so we can drink as much as we want. Sasha left you with all her bachelorette party stuff. We put it all in your room along with all her wedding stuff."

Sasha is the maid of honor who broke her leg. I hope my smile doesn't look forced as we go to my room, and sure enough, my bags are already there, courtesy of West. I just wish he was here with them.

"We'll let you get ready. In an hour, we're meeting the car down where we met you. Look hot!" Mandy says, and everyone goes their own way. I step into my room and take a deep breath. I know West is getting ready for the bachelor party, and I just hope it's not a strip club, but I don't want to sound like the insecure girlfriend either.

Taking some time, I go through the stuff from Sasha, and thankfully she was super organized. All the bachelorette party stuff seems to be in one bag, so I set it on the bed, and then get ready.

Putting on some music, I dress in the strapless formfitting gold dress I picked out for tonight. This was a pre-West dress choice, and I love that it has a mesh over the dress and has a ton of gold glitter, making it perfect for a bachelorette party. It has enough push=up to make my boobs look great too.

After I put some curls in my hair and do my makeup, I start second-guessing the dress. I was single when I packed it and had planned to be single when I wore it.

Quickly I take the photo of me already dressed and decide to send it to West.

Me: My dress was a pre-you choice. Don't be mad.

West: Fuck, you look hot. Why don't you wear that on one of our dates?

Me: Because it's not what I usually wear. It's way over the top.

West: And sexy as hell. Every guy will be looking at you tonight.

Me: Well, I won't be looking at them.

West: What are the bachelorette party plans?

I know he's trying to make sure we're going someplace decent. But I also give myself the perfect in to find out their plans too.

Me: Dinner and a wine bar. What about you?

When his response doesn't come, I start to wonder if my suspicion of them hitting a strip club is true.

***

Weston

Nate has been glued to my side since we got here, and it's made it hard to even text Rory without raising suspicion.

When I finally get a moment to check her text, I feel relief that they aren't going somewhere crazy for the bachelorette party. Because that dress screams 'fuck me,' and that's exactly what I want to do to her tonight in that dress.

Me: We are going to some local pool hall, a bar downtown.

Even as I get ready and meet the rest of the guys downstairs, I'm still checking my phone for a text from Rory, only to find nothing. Once in the car, I decide to text her again, but first, I change her name on my phone, just in case, to My Girl.

Me: Remember, you're mine, baby girl. No other guy touches.
My Girl: So long as you remember you're mine and no other girl touches you.
Me: Damn right I am, and I promise no one will touch me.
My Girl: No one will touch me either.

"Get your nose out of the phone!" Nate says, pulling my attention away. "What's so important?"

"Nothing, sorry." I try to focus on Nate because we are here for him.

Once at the pool hall, the guys start flirting with the waitresses who are in short shorts and cleavage-revealing tops. We order drinks and the waitresses start flirting back. I'm sure to increase tips once they heard it was a bachelor party. Nevertheless, I step back and keep space between them and me.

There is no problem with the guys having their fun, but I want no part in it. My phone goes off and with the guys distracted, I check it again.

My Girl: The girls were drunk before we even got in the car. This is going to be a long night.

Me: Some of the guys started drinking in their rooms too. I miss you already. Is it too soon for that?

My Girl: I hope not because I miss you too.

When our drinks get here, I tuck my phone away, and we start playing. The guys are drinking and getting loud and rowdy. I just keep to myself, play some pool and chat when one of the guys comes over.

Two games in, Nate comes to stand by me, watching the others with me.

"Something is different about you, but I just can't put my finger on it," he says.

I know Rory wants to give Nate and Mandy their day, but if we have this talk now, maybe we don't have to hide until after the wedding. Here we're a few hours into this, and I'm already going crazy without her. But this is what she wants.

"We can talk after the wedding. This weekend is about you." I tell him, thinking he'll drop it.

I should know better. I've known Nate for how long now? Of course, he isn't going to drop it.

"No, if something is going on, we need to talk now. I may be getting married, but you're my best friend, and that's important too." He moves further away from the other guys to give us a bit of privacy.

I hesitate. While I know Rory doesn't want to do this now, but if there is a chance we can spend this wedding together, I have to take it. I want to be with her. Just the few hours this evening having to pretend she isn't mine is killing me and I know I can't keep this up for several more days.

It's easier to ask forgiveness than ask permission. That's what my dad always says, despite my mom not liking it. But as I got older, I realized it's true and even more so right now.

"Something changed on the drive here with Rory. She isn't your little sister anymore. Well, I mean, she is, but she's an adult, she's grown up, smart, and beautiful. Though you didn't know it, I've always had a crush on her, but nothing came of it." I watch as his face hardens, but he hasn't said anything, so maybe it's a good thing.

"I want to date her. Not just as a fling. My feelings grew these last two weeks. I don't think I can stay away from her anymore, man. She's, my Mandy. I think I always knew it but was scared to act on it."

Nate still says nothing, but if looks could kill, this would for sure be lethal.

"My answer is no." Then he walks away and leaves me there.

Of all the ways I thought this might turn out, this wasn't it. Then I realize what I said.

"Nate, wait." He stops but doesn't turn toward me.

"We already started dating on the trip," I say, wanting to be upfront with him.

He looks over his shoulder, and thankfully we are still far enough from the other guys that they don't hear what's going on.

"My answer doesn't change. You and her, not going to happen."

This time when he walks away, I let him. We have already happened. So much so that there is no going back. But right now, there is no going forward, and I have no idea what the hell I'm going to do.

What I do know is I can't stay here. I leave and get a cab back to the vineyard, and head straight to my room.

I have to tell Rory before she finds out from Nate or Mandy, but also don't want to ruin her night.

Me: Let me know when you get back to your room. Hope your night is going better than mine.

Then I lay there and wait. I know I can't ruin Nate's wedding, which means essentially keeping this on the down low for the time being. But can I move forward at all with Nate saying no? He's my best friend, and we have been through some tough shit together.

But I love Rory, and I can't see myself walking away from her either.

What the fuck am I going to do?

Chapter 10

Rory

What a freakin' night. The girls just kept getting drunker and drunker. I didn't know you could get so drunk off wine alone, but these girls are living proof you can.

Of course, the tattoo Sasha had for the bridal party to wear on our wrists that said, "I'm with Mandy's Bachelorette party. If you find me, buy me a drink" didn't help. The guys were buying the girls' drinks left and right.

As the sober one, I made sure they got to their rooms, but to say I didn't have fun was an understatement. But I'll get my fun tomorrow when they are all hungover, and I get to mess with them all day. It's the small things, right?

I finally make it back to my room and check my phone.

Weston: Let me know when you get back to your room. Hope your night is going better than mine.

Me: I doubt my night was much better. Who knew you could get so drunk off of wine?

Weston: You're back in your room?

Me: Yep, just got here, and my feet are thanking me for taking my heels off.

Weston: Have you been drinking?

Me: No, not a big wine person.

Weston: I'm on my way.

That's what I'm talking about. The perfect way to relax is in his arms. I check my hair and makeup to make sure they are still halfway decent, and thankfully they are. But I leave the dress on because I hope he was thinking about me in it all night. I know I've been thinking of him peeling it off of me.

There is a soft knock on my door, and I open it, and West walks in. When he closes the door behind him, I expect him to pin me to it, but he doesn't. So, I move to him and wrap my arms around his neck and pull him in for a kiss.

When his whole body tenses up, I stop. Something happened tonight. Something he doesn't want to tell me but has to because I'll find out from someone else.

"What happened, West?" I take a step back from him. "Did you guys end up at a strip club?"

"Nothing like that. In fact, I left the pool hall early and came back to my room, *alone.*"

I relax knowing it wasn't a girl, so it can't be too bad, right?

"Then what is it?"

He runs a hand through his hair, then turns and starts pacing the room.

"Nate hadn't had as much to drink as I thought. He pulled me aside and noticed I was distracted by my phone. Then he said I was different. You know how he is. Even when I said it was no big deal and we could talk after the wedding, he wouldn't drop it."

I start to get a sinking feeling in my stomach. He wouldn't have told Nate, right? I asked him not to, and we agreed to this.

"He kept pushing, and I hated being away from you tonight, so I took a chance. I told him I want to date you, that I'm serious about you and that we had started a relationship on the trip."

I wait for him to go on, but he doesn't.

"What did Nate say?"

"He said no. That you and I aren't going to happen."

He won't even look me in the eye now, which isn't like West.

"I didn't say anything, just let him walk away. That wasn't the place to make a scene."

"Okay, then you will be at his room first thing in the morning and talk to him. Get this worked out before it goes any further."

"This has been on my mind all night, and like you said, we don't want to ruin the wedding. So, let's just let it be, and I'll work it out with Nate. He needs to cool off and think about this. Maybe we should take a pause and get through the wedding. I'm going to make this right."

I refuse to let West see me cry, so I beeline right to the bathroom and lock myself in just as the tears start pouring down my face. So many thoughts are racing through my head.

West said he loved me but now wants a break to make my brother happy. He's letting my brother control us. Nate is being an asshole. What the hell is he thinking? I can't believe I agreed to be the fill-in maid of honor. If I knew, I wouldn't have agreed. I don't care if the wedding is ruined. If Nate can be selfish, so can I.

"I'll make this right," Weston says right before I hear the door to my room close.

I grab a makeup wipe and clear off my make-up even though it doesn't help matters much. My face is red and blotchy from crying.

Going to my bed, I grab my phone and call Kinsley because I need to talk to someone, and there is no one here to talk to. No one else knows about us.

I tell her everything through big sobs and lots of tears, and she listens to every bit of it.

"What am I going to do?"

"Want me to send my sister out there to junk punch them both? You know she's always up for putting a guy in their place."

"Though the idea is temping at least for Nate, anyway. Right now, I don't want to be the maid of honor or even be at this wedding. I can't act happy that my brother gets his happily ever after when he is stopping me from getting mine."

"Well, the maid of honor is for Mandy, and she did nothing wrong. Don't hold this against her. As for the rest, you don't have to be happy, you just have to be there. Then as soon as it's over, just come home. We can do a girl's night binge, watch some *Pretty Woman,* and down some ice cream, and things will start to look better."

"I just wish for once I was someone's first choice."

***

Rory

I'm getting ready for the rehearsal dinner tonight, and of course, the girls all decided they wanted to make it an event. So here we are in Mandy's bridal suite, which is like a huge one-bedroom apartment, getting dressed.

The girls have been laughing and joking about the bachelorette party last night, and I can't even muster up a smile. Even though I'm trying really hard, the best I can do is show up. Last night I cried on the phone for an hour with Kinsley. Then when I got off the phone, I cried myself to sleep.

I'm paying for it now because my eyes are puffy, and I look like hell. At the moment, I don't care how I look. But someday, when I look back at Nate and Mandy's wedding pictures, when and if I actually forgive my brother, I'm going to hate that I looked a mess. But that day is so far in the future I'm finding it hard to care about it.

While all the girls are scattered in the bathroom and bedroom using every available mirror, I'm in the living room trying to get some space. If I want to listen, I can still hear the conversation, but right now, I don't.

Until Mandy sits down next to me on the couch.

"What's wrong?" she asks.

I force a smile and shake my head but keep my eyes on the mirror I have in front of me.

"Come on. I know something is wrong. You can't get far enough away from anything fun.

Your eyes look like you cried yourself to sleep, and you haven't smiled once."

"I'm fine, really." I manage to get out.

"Is this the reason Nate has been acting really off since last night too?" Mandy asks, and that is when I lose it.

I start crying, and she instantly pulls me into a hug.

"All right, everyone out. Take your shit and go to your own rooms." Mandy hollers, and everyone starts scrambling as I continue to cry on her shoulder. Thankfully, she is still in a t-shirt and not the beautiful dress she is wearing tonight.

Once the tears start, I can't seem to get them to stop. You would think I cried them all out last night, but apparently not because they just keep coming. As everyone leaves, Mandy holds me, rubbing my back. Once we have the suite to ourselves, she grabs a cloth and wipes my face.

"Ok now, what is going on?"

"I didn't want this to ruin your wedding. I swear we weren't going to even bring it up until after, but Nate has a way..."

"Of picking at things until they gush open and bleed all over the place? Yeah, I noticed, and we are working on it," Mandy says.

I nod and take a sip of my water.

"As you know, I had planned to take that trip alone. It's been on my bucket list since I was in middle school and heard about Route 66.

I had it all planned out. Then Nate called me thanks to your true-crime show addiction, and he didn't want me to go alone. Thanks for that, by the way," I smirk at her. My first genuine somewhat smile all day.

"I like watching him squirm when I remind him I know a hundred ways they will never find his body if he cheats on me," Mandy shrugs.

"Nate would never. He's so in love with you." I reassure her.

She shrugs and smiles because it's true. "So, he makes West go on the trip with you."

"Yes," I continue. "I had a crush on West for years but never acted on it because he's Nate's best friend. Only I didn't know West had a crush on me, too. We found out on the trip, and we took things to a logical conclusion. Since we already knew each other so well, by the time we reached California we were head over heels for each other."

"I'm so excited for you! West is a great guy!" She says with a huge smile, but then it falls. "What happened?"

"Last night, Nate cornered West at the pool hall because he didn't want the girls all over him, and he was texting me. Nate wanted to know what was going on with him, and he wouldn't drop it."

"Typical Nate," Mandy says.

"So, West told him. He wanted to date me, that he already was, and it was serious."

"What did Nate say?" Mandy grits out from between clenched teeth. She already knows but wants me to confirm it.

"He said it's not happening. After that, West left the pool hall early, and after I got you and the girls to your rooms last night, he met me in my room and said he wants a 'pause'" I use air quotes and then grab a tissue because, dammit, there are more tears.

"He wants to make things right with Nate before moving forward. All this 'you're mine and let me worry about Nate' shit the whole trip, and bam, I'm put on pause while Nate gets his happily ever after. I'm sorry. I love you and want you as my sister. But I just can't be happy for Nate right now." I barely get the last part out as I burst into tears again.

I'm going to be a blubbering mess tonight, and there is no way I can get out of it. Everyone expects me to be there, including Mom and Dad. I really don't want to have this conversation with my mom. She isn't above dragging us by our ears and locking us in a room until we work it out, even if it means we both miss the wedding.

"You let me deal with Nate. He needs me to talk some sense into him, and I think a rude awakening that the world doesn't revolve around him," Mandy says.

"I can't let you do that. It's your wedding." I shake my head.

"You can and you will because it is my wedding. We're about to be family, and I know you have never had a sister, but this is what sisters do."

She hugs me tight, and for that brief moment, I feel okay, that is until I have to go into the rehearsal dinner.

Chapter 11

Weston

I haven't been able to take my eyes off Rory since the rehearsal. She looks stunning in her simple navy blue cocktail dress. The problem? She hasn't looked at me once.

Her eyes are slightly puffy, not something you'd notice unless you have every detail of her body memorized as I do. It's a sign she's been crying, and it guts me that I caused this. I just don't know how to fix it.

I want to be over there with her, holding her, not across the room or across the table. The reception dinner is outside in the vineyard. There is a long table set for the wedding party to enjoy. It's romantic the way they have lights strung up overhead like a canopy. It would have been nice to eat with Rory and enjoy the ambiance.

As I start to make my way over to Rory to talk, Nate stops me with a frown.

"Dad wants to hear about your trip," he says in a flat voice.

He knows I was going to talk to Rory, and now he's going to do everything he can to stop me. I sigh, go talk to his dad, and before I know it, everyone is being pushed to the table to sit down and eat.

Mandy and Nate are at the head of the table, and Mandy's smile looks strained. I wonder if she knows what's going on. She's very good at picking up on things, so it wouldn't surprise me if she's put two and two together and then dragged it from Nate. I wonder what her thoughts on all this are, but I don't dare ask.

The food gets passed around, and people start toasting Mandy and Nate. I know as best man I'll have to speak eventually, as will Rory, now that she's the maid of honor. But Nate beats us to it.

Nate stands and gets everyone's attention by tapping his fork to his champagne glass, and the clinking sound quiets the table.

"You may not know that Rory is the reason we are all here today." While his smile looks a bit forced, he won't even look at Rory. I'm wondering where this is going because I don't know how Rory fit into how he met Mandy.

"I was on a business trip here in California, and Rory had just broken up with a guy. She called me needing to talk because her best friend was at some work thing and had her phone off. So, I left the hotel and went for a walk on the beach. It was almost sunset, and I was looking down at the water washing over my feet when I ran into Mandy, literally ran into her."

When he looks over at Mandy, the smile on his face is genuine, and you can see the love there.

"I was so tongue-tied and if you know me, that has never happened. Mandy was jogging on the beach in these short shorts and a black and pink sports bra, her hair pulled back in a ponytail, and I just remember thinking I'd never seen someone so beautiful. The sparks from our brief touch were unlike anything I'd ever felt before. As Mandy was jogging away, Rory told me I better go after her. We hung up, and that's what I did. We spent the rest of the night at a beachside bar talking, and well, the rest is history."

I look over at Rory and she's fuming. Even though I can see it, I don't expect her to stand up and go off on her brother.

"I might have reconsidered if I had known you were going to stop me from my happiness." Then she storms off back toward the lobby where we are all staying.

No one says a word, but a quick glance at Nate shows he's pissed, and when Mandy and his parents stand up, I know things are about to get even worse.

Mandy speaks first and doesn't even try to keep her voice down.

"Are you really willing to ruin our wedding to make your sister and best friend miserable? Do you really want to be that selfish?" Mandy asks.

"He isn't good enough for her." Nate grits out, and I feel like I've been punched in the face. My best friend doesn't think I'm good enough.

"He was a player in high school and not much better in college," Nate tries to justify his answer.

"But he isn't now," Mandy says.

"I haven't been with anyone since our senior year in college. Ever ask yourself why?" I finally stand up and speak out. Nate's eyes land on me, so I keep talking.

"It was the year I went with your family to the cabin for Christmas. You brought your then-girlfriend, and I ended up with Rory at every event because we were the third wheel to you and your parents. We were forced together for everything, and I fell in love with her then, and I barely kept it together. But this trip you forced us on? It was too much. I wasn't that strong, but I don't regret it. Yes, I love her." I say louder than I mean to.

The rest of the people at the table start whispering. Most of them are Mandy's family and the bridal party, who don't know Nate and me very well. Who knows what they're thinking, but for sure, they're getting a great show.

"So, help me, Nate. You make this right, or I won't marry you." Mandy says, then storms off in the direction Rory went.

Nate shoots an icy glare at me, and I brace myself for whatever he has to say. Only his mom gets to him first. She grabs his ear and yanks his head down by her mouth and starts talking so low no one hears her, but you can tell she's mad. His father stands next to his mother with his arms crossed, ready to defend his wife from anyone who tries to step up.

No matter how mad Nate is, my path is suddenly clear.

I need to find Rory and beg her to forgive me. I'm an idiot.

***

Rory

I walk out of the reception dinner pissed and hurt. What the hell was my brother thinking bringing up the moment where I was unselfish and led him to his happily ever after? Did he really think I'd be okay with it after what he did? Maybe he was just pushing my buttons, or maybe he was trying to appease me. Who knows what he wanted.

The more I think it over, the more the hurt shifts to anger. How dare he get his happily ever after while preventing mine! Who the hell does he think he is? How dare West take his side on all this! Fuck them both. I scream in my head, though I know I don't mean it.

It hurts. I want to be someone's first choice. I want someone to look my brother in the eye and say, 'I'm sorry you feel that way, but I'm still going to date her.' How hard is that? West said he loved me, but I guess that love is conditional on my brother's approval. How stupid was I?

God, I'd give anything for Kinsley to be here right now, to have someone unconditionally on my side. Mandy has been great, but I know her loyalty is with Nate in the end.

I think back to that night Nate met Mandy. When I found out Jimmy the Jerk was cheating on me, I was heartbroken. I felt stupid that I hadn't seen it before. Kinsley was flying to some business retreat and was in the air, and I couldn't call her, so I called my brother.

I needed him but knew he might have something special with Mandy, and I encouraged him to go after her. He was going to let her walk away to be there for me, but I didn't let him. Stupid me, right?

As I'm on my way to my room, I realize that is where everyone would go looking for me. So instead, I walk the grounds, and when I turn the corner there's a small wood bridge going over a creek. It's got great views of the vineyard, and it's on the opposite side from where the rehearsal dinner is, so I stop here to gather my thoughts.

I don't know how long I'm there, but it must be a while because suddenly someone is beside me. Looking up, I find my dad.

"How did you find me?"

"I know you, sweetheart. Before you talked to anyone, you would go for a walk to clear your head."

I rest my head on my dad's shoulder, and even though we're on the other side of the country, it still feels like home. I wait for whatever lecture he has for me, about how I should have better control of my emotions since this weekend is about Nate. I deserve it, I know I do.

"I've never heard your mother cuss one of you kids out until today. If you could have heard what she said to your brother." Daddy shakes his head.

"What?" I lift my head in shock.

"Oh yeah, your mother was pissed. The only time I've ever heard her cuss like that was during childbirth back when there was no pain medication," he chuckles.

I don't think I've heard a single cuss word ever come from my mother's mouth in anger, much less her swear at anyone.

"Your brother was wrong to say what he did." Dad wraps his arm around my shoulders.

"It doesn't matter. West put us on hold anyway because Nate's opinion is more important than his love for me." Even though I mumble, I know dad heard every word.

"Did West say that?"

"No."

"Then you need to give him the benefit of the doubt. I think he was worried because he knows how close you and Nate are and didn't want to get between that. He's so hell-bent on fixing things for you that he isn't seeing it your way. The same way you aren't seeing it his way."

"Whose side are you on?" I shove my shoulder against his.

"Always yours. Just don't tell your brother. West is like a second son to me, and I approve of him for you. I watched him grow up. He's a good guy, but even we good guys screw things up. Take some time to cool off but let him back in."

I sigh, "Maybe."

That's the best I can give my dad right now, and he knows it, so he doesn't push. He just kisses the top of my head and heads back to the wineary.

Sitting there for a while longer, I let my dad's words run through my head. At some point, I'll forgive West, but not tonight, not this weekend.

Finally, I pull my phone out of my bag and see I have twenty-six missed calls, most from West, some from Mandy, Nate, and my mom. I have over forty texts too. I flip through those.

Nate: This is not the same, and you know it.
Nate: We need to talk about this.
Nate: Why West? Of all the guys, why him? Have you thought about what will happen when this ends badly?

Not if, but when. He's so sure I'll fuck this up. Tears swim in my eyes before I wipe them away.

Mom: I'll deal with your brother. Let me know you are okay.

My mom, I text back.

Me: I'm fine. Talked to Dad. Going back to my room now.

I debate deleting West's texts, and I almost do, but I know my dad won't be happy if I don't at least glance at them.

West: Hey you, okay?
West: Where are you?
West: Can we talk?
West: I'm so sorry. Please talk to me.
West: This is all my fault. Let me fix it.

There are a bunch of texts from him all asking about the same thing, but it's the last one that breaks me.

West: Baby girl, please tell me you're okay.

The nickname he's been using the last two weeks. The one he hasn't used since we got here. It's too much.

I can't do this.

Chapter 12

Weston

Where the hell is Rory? She isn't in her room or anyplace in the building. No one has seen her. I have to know she is okay.

I screwed up big time, and I now not only risk losing my best friend but also the love of my life. That Christmas senior year, I knew she was someone special, but fuck two weeks? And now I know I want to marry this girl and spend the rest of my life with her.

I need to find her and tell her that. I knew it tonight. Nothing else matters but her. I don't care about Nate, her parents, or my parents. I just need her. We can make new friends, or we'll start our own family, but if she walks away, she takes my heart and soul with her.

In a last-ditch attempt to find her, I start checking the ladies' bathrooms. When I still can find her, I send her another text message.

West: Baby girl, please tell me you're okay.

I check the back porch again, and this is where Nate finds me. I'm so not in the mood to do this. Whereas last night I was ready to let him punch me and get it over with, tonight I'm ready to punch him. So, for his benefit, I start talking before he does.

"Listen, I started falling for her that Christmas senior year of college. I haven't been with anyone since. Not to date and not to sleep with. I just knew she was it, but I didn't see it happening, so I kept waiting for someone better, but there never was. Until this trip, which was, by the way, your idea, I didn't touch her." I throw it back at him because he isn't completely at fault in this.

He opens his mouth to talk, and I stop him.

"I love her. I love her so damn much that this is killing me. You're pissed at me and weren't talking to me before now, I can deal with that. But she's pissed and not talking to me and that I can't handle. If I have to pick, then I pick her. I'm sorry, man, but I can't lose her. As soon as I can get her to forgive me, I'm going to marry her. I hope you'll forgive me, but if not, then so be it."

Staring him down, I wait to see what his next move is.

"I want to punch you so bad, but Mandy would kill me for ruining the wedding photos.

So, when I get back from my honeymoon, be ready. I'm not going easy on you. You cheat on her, and it will be the last thing you ever do. Best friend or not, I got people who will dump your body so far offshore it will never be found."

I nod because I don't doubt that he would just do it himself. If I hurt her like that, I'd gladly offer myself up for anything he dishes out.

"Now go find her and make this right so I can get married." He punches me in the shoulder hard enough to make me stumble back a foot.

"I'm trying to find her, but I'm out of places to look."

He just gives me a pointed glare and walks off.

After I do another sweep of the building, but I still can't find her. She isn't replying to my messages or calls. Then I sit in the lobby and think. I know she wouldn't leave, mostly because she doesn't have a car.

When she was younger, and she would get upset about something, she'd go for a walk. But I saw her come toward the building. She wouldn't have stayed outside when that's where everyone else was.

Resting my elbow on my knees, I put my head in my hands and stare at the ground and think. My brain is empty until someone sits down next to me. I look up to find Rory's dad.

"Men build too many walls and not enough bridges. Joseph Newton said that, and it couldn't be truer. Go build a bridge, son." He pats my shoulder and then stands with a wink at me and goes upstairs.

Well, I never thought I'd see the day the old man finally lost his marbles. I get that he's being philosophical and all, but how does that help me find...

Then I remember Nate saying something about photos being taken on the other bridge tomorrow. After rushing up to the front desk and asking about the bridge not being used by the wedding, I get directed to the side of the building.

As I follow the path, I'm hoping maybe her dad was giving me a hint without betraying his daughter's trust. Sure enough, when I walk around the curve there is a bridge going over a small creek, and on it stands Rory,

I almost collapse in relief that she's okay and that I found her. Her dad I owe big time for this. Standing still for a moment, I simply watch her. She is looking at her phone, and I'm sure seeing all the missed calls and texts for the first time. The light on her phone hits her face, and even from here, I can see the tears on her face.

Tears I put there. It feels like someone is trying to rip out my heart. Anything I can do to stop the tears, to make sure she doesn't cry again for as long as I live, I'll do. She shuts her phone off and puts it away. When she turns towards me to head back to the winery, that's when she sees me.

She stops, not even off the bridge yet, and we both stare at each other.

I slowly start walking toward her, never once taking my eyes from her. She watches my every move, and it isn't long until I'm standing right in front of her.

This is it. It's make or break time.

***

Rory

I tuck my phone away and take one last look out over the vineyard before I turn to go back to my room. Only that is when I spot West watching me from a little further up the path. Our eyes lock, and those stupid feelings are still there.

Be strong, I remind myself. My heart says that's no problem with how much it's hurting. As he walks closer, I debate running the other way, but it's dark, and I don't know where I'd go.

Once West is in front of me, he falls to his knees and takes my hands in his.

"It's always been you. I love you and have for a long time now."

My heart starts to heal, and I almost give in. But then he says one more thing.

"Now I have your brother's permission."

There it is, the bucket of cold water. He isn't doing this because he can't live without me. He isn't doing this because he chose me and said consequences be damned. He's doing it because he got my brother's permission. Permission he only got because he got called out in front of everyone, and Mom probably made him do it.

The tears start, and I don't even bother to stop them or wipe them away.

"Do you understand how much it hurts to be cast aside because of someone else's opinion? Especially after everything we said and did?" I pull my hands from his.

"For once, I want to be someone's first choice. The choice they make because nothing else matters. I'm done. Now put on a smile, and let's get them married. I just want to go home."

With that, I walk past him and right to my room without even looking back.

By the time I get to my room, I've gotten the tears to stop, and thankfully I didn't run into anyone on the way. Only my luck is short-lived when I open the door and find Mandy sitting in the middle of the bed waiting on me.

"Do I even want to know how you got in here?"

She shrugs, "Your brother made a mess of it. I told him to use his money and get me in here. And he did. I also made him pay for two of the most expensive bottles of wine, and we're going to drink them and go over all the ways he's an idiot."

"I'm sure this isn't how you planned the night before your wedding," I grumble and take my shoes off.

"Spending it with the girl who will officially be my sister tomorrow when she needs me is exactly what I want to do. Spending your brother's money is a bonus."

"I'm sorry for all this." I sigh and sit down next to her.

She hugs me tight, "It keeps things fun, and it will be something I can hold over his head forever. Oh, I can't go to Hawaii? Remember when you almost ruined our wedding... He will never live it down. This is it great!" she laughs.

"Now go change while I open the first bottle." She shoos me off the bed. I change into my comfy sweatpants and one of West's t-shirts I stole from him. The cat's out of the bag, so no point in hiding it.

Before heading out of the bathroom, I make a call and move my plane ticket up to the red-eye tomorrow night so I can leave right after the wedding instead of the next day. I know West will be on the plane with me if I don't and I can't be trapped a mile in the air for several hours with him right now.

When I come back out, Mandy hands me a bottle of wine. Then I tell her everything from the walk I took, to my talk with my dad, and West finding me, and then finally, me walking away.

"I don't blame you one bit. I want to be someone's first choice, too," she says.

We finish off one bottle of wine before she turns to me.

"Do you want to be alone right now?" she asks.

"Not really."

"Good, let's open this second bottle and rent a movie. Want me to call down and see if they have ice cream?"

"Can I trade Nate for you? I'd rather have you for a sister them him for brother right now."

She hugs me. "I am your sister always. Even after I get married, if your brother is being an idiot like we all know he can be, you can come to me, and we can vent and just be. I'm always going to be here for you."

"I better call Kinsley and fill her in." I sigh, realizing it's after midnight back in Chicago.

"Call her. I'll order ice cream and find a rom-com for us to watch when you're done."

As I call Kinsley, I watch Mandy text on her phone. I'm sure she's telling everyone I'm okay and where she'll be tonight. When her face turns angry while texting, I know she is texting my brother. Even though she's mad, I can still see her love for him.

Someday. I tell myself. Someday I'll find that.

"I knew I should have sent my sister. Those men need a good ball kicking," Kinsley says.

"Right now, I can't agree with you more. I changed my plane ticket to the red-eye tomorrow night after the wedding, so I'll be home earlier than expected."

"Good. Go home, sleep as long as you want and then when you wake up, call me. I'll bring food, ice cream, and margaritas."

"Sounds perfect." I hang up just as room service gets here, and not only did Mandy order ice cream, but there is also chocolate cake too.

She hands me another glass of wine.

"Confession. I hate wine, but right now, knowing how much this is costing Nate, it's my favorite drink in the world." I smile and take a sip.

Then Mandy starts laughing. "Is that why you didn't drink at the bachelorette party? I wish you had said something. I'd have found you a drink!"

"It's fine. Who would have helped you girls to bed if I had been drinking?"

Just like that, we launch into giggles as we eat ice cream and watch TV. I start to feel better, and as much as I dislike Nate right now, I'm glad he's marrying Mandy and making her part of the family.

I just have to get through tomorrow.

Chapter 13

Weston

I've been on edge, wanting to see Rory all day. I tried several times, but Mandy has the bridesmaids keeping me so far away I can't even catch a glance.

I barely slept last night. If it weren't for the text from Nate telling me Mandy was with her last night, I would have been pounding her door down to make sure she made it back to her room okay.

At least I'll see her soon. We're walking down the aisle together, so she can't avoid me forever. Also, we're getting pictures taken, sitting at the same table, and having one required dance together. Today I plan to make the most of my time.

I need to grovel and tell her what an idiot I am and beg for another chance. Hell, I'll settle for the hint of another chance.

Last night I thought I was on the verge of getting her back. The tears had stopped, and she was smiling. Until stupid me went and brought up having her brother's permission. While I should have known that would set her off, I wasn't thinking like that.

Though I had thought she'd be happy I settled things with her brother but seeing it from her point of view, I now realize I handled this all wrong. Normally I'd talk to Nate about it, but that isn't an option for obvious reasons, so I sat down with Rory's dad at breakfast this morning.

He was guarded, and I don't blame him, seeing as how we are talking about his daughter. But he said he understands her point of view and understands mine and is not sure what he would have done in my shoes, which isn't very reassuring.

Actually, I just needed him to know I was going to fight for her. I may have also told him that if the right time came up, I was going to ask her to marry me. He stared me down, and that conversation is one I won't forget.

"Shouldn't you be asking for my blessing instead of telling me you plan to do it?" he asked.

"Well, asking for someone's approval is what got me in this mess, so no. I'm not asking, I'm giving you a heads up."

For a solid minute, he confronted me with his stare, and when I didn't back down, he smiled.

"Looks like you learned your lesson. For the record, you have always had my blessing. Nate might be an idiot, but there is no one I trust my little girl with more than you."

It took everything in me not to cry then, and even now, my eyes mist thinking about it.

It's then the wedding planner comes in and gathers the groomsmen, and gets us in place as we wait on the bridesmaids to join us.

She goes over what we're to do yet again like we weren't told twenty times at the rehearsal last night. Then the bridesmaids walk down and join us on the back patio. Their dresses are a deep wine red, which goes perfectly with a fall wedding at a vineyard.

But as they take their places, there is no sign of Rory, and I start to worry, but the wedding planner isn't concerned. Mandy isn't here yet either, so maybe there is some maid of honor things they are taking care of at the last minute.

Another glance into the lobby, and that's when I see her walking out with Mandy. Her dress is the same deep wine red, and it's one of those off-the-shoulder ones. Tight at the top but loose and flowy from the waist down. She looks drop-dead gorgeous.

They step out on the patio, and Rory's smile fades when she sees me, and my heart feels like it's being ripped from my chest. When she stands next to me, she puts enough space between us that another person could stand there.

The wedding planner goes over instructions again, and then the music starts, and the first couple starts down the aisle. We have a long way to walk. It's down the path, over a small bridge, and to the area of the vineyard the wedding ceremony will take place. Today I'm grateful for that long walk.

When it's finally our turn, I hold my arm out to her, and she takes it but is very stiff and still puts as much distance between us as possible. Once we begin walking, I try to talk to her.

"Will you please hear me out?" I whisper even though there is no one around to hear us.

"No. Today is about Mandy, not you."

"I wasn't thinking. I thought if I smoothed things over with Nate..."

"West, for the love of God. Shut. Up."

I'm stunned speechless. Rory always has a kind word for everyone, and I have only seen her lose her temper twice in the twenty years I've known her. For her to act like this, I know I fucked up on a major scale. In the effort to not make it worse, I do as she asks and don't speak, but place my free hand over hers that's on my arm.

It's a silent show of support, and I hope it lets her know I'm there for her. What I want her to know is I'm not going anywhere, no matter how much she tries to push me away. Even though I don't want to let go of her when we reach Nate and the minister, I do, and then my eyes stay on her.

I don't see Mandy walk up the aisle, and I don't hear the wedding vows. All I see is Rory in that sexy bridesmaid dress. The smile she has on is fake, but the tears in her eyes are real, and I want to rush to her side and hold her, tell her everything will be okay, but I know she would kill me.

When the ceremony is over, she walks up to me, and we walk down the aisle.

"Not. A. Word." She says, and the moment we're back at the winery she disappears.

I'm so fucked.

***

Rory

The second the wedding was over, I took the coward's way out and ran and hid in a storage closet. Being so close to West like that was hell on my nerves, and my body didn't care that we were mad at him. It still wanted him desperately.

The more he talked, the more I felt my resistance give way, and I couldn't break down during the wedding, so the best thing was for him not to talk. Now I still have the pictures and the reception to get through, but I can do this.

As Kinsley always coaches me, I try to calm my breathing and recenter myself. Finally, my heartbeat slows and I start to feel calmer. My bags are packed and ready to go, and my outfit is lying on my bed. The second this reception is over, I'm out of here. When I get home, I'll have some space from West. And hopefully, get some clarity.

That's what I need, space to think without running into him around every corner.

A few more deep breaths and I head out to stand for photos. Thankfully, many of the photos are guys on one side and girls on the other, which means West is always at least two people away from me in each pose.

Then the photographer suggests a couples photo. I look at Mandy, pleading for her to say no, but she gives me a sad smile as if to say I'm sorry and agrees. West wastes no time and steps up behind me and wraps his arms around my waist, pressing his chest to my back as the photographer instructs.

He sighs in relief and places a kiss on the top of my head. Stupid me actually feels safe in his arms and likes being here. Between photos, he leans down and whispers in my ear.

"I know you don't want to be here taking these pictures with me, but having you in my arms is the highlight of my day, baby girl, even if you are mad at me. We might fight, but I'm not walking away. I'm going to fight for you, for us."

It's too much, and I don't care what photos Mandy has planned. I break free from his arms and run back inside, back to the storage closet and take some deep breaths. When I'm calm again, I go out to the reception and play the game of avoiding Nate and West while not getting so drunk that they won't let me on my flight.

I do well until it's time to sit down and eat, and West is at the same table as me. We're set to sit next to each other, but I move the place cards around and sit across from him. He doesn't take his eyes off me the entire dinner. With his gaze on me, I feel his eyes burning my skin.

For the rest of the dinner, I manage only to look his way twice when the groomsmen next to him were asking me questions.

Once dinner is over, the dancing starts. After Nate and Mandy's first dance, I have to take my turn with West.

As he pulls me in his arms, I try to keep as much space between us as possible.

"You know I almost asked you to prom? But Nate set me up with Cindy," he says.

"Well, he wouldn't have let you take me anyway, and you would have done as he said," I throw back.

"I hate that our first dance is like this. I want to pull you close, kiss you in front of everyone, and see that smile I miss so much."

Without answering him, I look off to the side. He sighs but doesn't push it, thankfully.

The song ends, and he lets me go only for the brother and sister dance to be announced. I curse under my breath, causing West to chuckle.

"Give him hell, baby girl." He leaves me on the dance floor as Nate joins me.

"This was Mandy's idea," he says.

"Figures."

If I thought dancing with West was awkward, that was ballroom-worthy compared to dancing with Nate. Neither of us says anything for the first part of the song.

"I do want you to be happy." He finally says.

"Funny way of showing it."

"Why West?"

"Why Mandy?"

His eyes meet mine, and after a moment, he nods.

"We can't help who we fall in love with. I know. It's just hard. He's always been my best friend, and I feel like I'm losing him."

"Because you're pushing him away. Instead of being happy for him and supporting him, look at what you're doing. Do you want this to be how you remember your wedding forever? There's still a chance to change it. Mandy has already said you'll never live it down. You have no chance of ever winning an argument because this is her trump card."

He smiles then, "Like I had any chance of winning an argument, anyway."

"Not with her. She's a great person. When she stayed with me last night, it felt like I had a sister. So don't screw this up because in the event of a divorce, I pick her."

"Gee, thanks for the support." he rolls his eyes.

"If you had supported West and me, I'd have your back, but payback is a bitch."

"I really am sorry."

"I know, and I'll forgive you. But right now, I just need this wedding to be over so I can go home and get some space and think."

"The cake cutting is next. If you want to duck out after that, I'll cover for you."

"Thanks." The song ends, and I give him a hug.

Though I had planned to stay mad at him for at least the rest of the night, I never could stay angry at him.

After they smash cake in each other's faces, Nate shoots me a wink, and I sneak out and back to my room to change. Then I call down to the lobby and request a ride.

I manage to get to the airport before getting a text asking where I am. Ignoring it, I head to my flight. I'll have an hour to kill, but I have some good books on my phone to read.

I thought getting space would help me breathe, so why am I still gasping for air?

Chapter 14

Weston

Everyone is enjoying their cake, but I can't find Rory anywhere. Thinking she might have ducked out to the restroom, I sit at the table and eat my cake and watch for her. When I still can't find her twenty minutes later, I get up to look for her to at least make sure she's okay.

But Nate catches up to me first.

"Have you seen Rory?" I ask.

I don't want to worry him, but they seemed okay after their dance. Maybe he knows where she is.

"She left man, and I didn't pry. But I was going to ask you what the fuck happened," he says as Mandy walks up beside him.

"What do you mean she left?" I ask.

"She changed her flight and left to go home early."

I have to go after her. As if Nate can read my mind, he grabs my arm.

"What happened? I thought you were going to fix this."

Running my hand through my hair, I sigh. Then I tell them what she said last night and while we were dancing. Mandy listens too, though I'm guessing she heard all this from Rory herself.

By the time I'm done talking, Nate's face is pale, and he actually looks shaken.

"She's right, you know," Mandy says to Nate, "You have always been a roadblock for every guy she has dated, and no guy has yet to pick her over you. So, I see her point."

She gestures between Nate and me. "Your loyalty has always been to each other. How can she trust either of you to be loyal to her and pick her? Especially you." She turns to me and stares me down.

This woman might be small, but she is damn scary. Then, without blinking, she just stares, waiting for me to talk. But since I have no answer for her, I only shake my head.

"If you want a relationship, she has to be first. No. Matter. What. I'm sorry but screw Nate."

"Hey!" Nate says, acting like he's offended, but I can see the smile he's trying to hide while staring at his new bride.

"Listen. Nate's your best friend, and he will forgive you later on, especially if he sees you treating Rory right. But you're risking losing her now, and if you don't fix this right away. Then there is no coming back from it."

Shit, she's right. Nate and I have been through some tough shit but didn't I decide just last night that I can live without Nate? But I can't live without her.

"I need to go after her," I say, making plans in my head.

"The next flight out isn't until tomorrow, anyway, and it's the one you're already booked on. Let her get home and have a bit of space to think. But you need to cool off and come up with a game plan," Mandy says.

I look back toward the reception and can't stomach the idea of going back in there.

"You okay if I go back to my room? I want to pack and get a game plan in place."

"Yeah, man, but I'm warning you. If this shit isn't fixed when we stop by after our honeymoon, I'll beat the shit out of you. Got it?" Nate says, and I know he's deadly serious.

"If I can't fix this by then, I'll welcome it." I hug him and kiss Mandy on the cheek before I beeline it to my room.

I check the flights, and sure enough, my flight is the next best way home. I could leave now and have three layovers, but I'd get in thirty minutes after my original flight. So as much as I hate to sit here and wait, that's what I plan to do.

Then I pull up her flight and track it on my screen. As I watch her get further and further away from me, I swear my heart is going with her. I feel the distance growing, and I can't stand it. There is no way I'm getting any sleep tonight.

Pacing the room watching Rory get further and further away, I'm no closer to a game plan. When she lands for her layover in Denver, I watch her connecting flight.

An hour later, the universe gives me a Hail Mary, and I swear I hear it say, don't fuck this one up.

***

Rory

What a freakin' mess. I hate leaving California and West behind, but I knew it was the right thing to do. I got to Denver where my layover was, and one thing after a freakin' another happened.

First, the flight was delayed by forty-five minutes due to the weather. That was fine. I went and got something to eat and a coffee. Then the plane we were supposed to fly on had some issues, so we had to wait for a new plane.

We're still thirty minutes away from boarding, so I call Kinsley and fill her in on the wedding. By the time I got to the airport last night, it was after midnight her time, and I didn't want to bother her.

"Wow. But he came back, so maybe don't write it off completely?" she says.

"I was supposed to be in bed by now, so I could think about all this."

"You would have been better off taking your original flight."

"With West. No, that wasn't an option. I couldn't sit next to him for hours. It was hard enough walking down the aisle and dancing with him."

No sooner do I get off the phone than they announce the flight has been delayed a third time to allow the flight crew to ready the plane. Everyone in the waiting area groans, and many let out a few curses.

Thankfully, that's the last delay, and before I know it, I'm in the air watching Chicago come into view. I don't remember the last time I've been so tired and emotionally drained. I feel like crying and screaming all at once, and I swear if one more thing goes wrong before I get home, I might punch someone in the face.

When we land, I don't think a plane has ever cleared out so quickly. We were all just done with this flight and the delays. I know it wasn't the flight crew's fault, but the cheery flight attendant saying goodbye to everyone was on the receiving end of many death stares.

Now, off to get my bags and go home. Only as I enter the area where family waits for those getting off the plane, there stands West, looking like he hasn't gotten any sleep either.

Great. So much for crawling into bed. Now I have to deal with him.

"What are you doing here?" I don't even bother to hide my irritation.

"I got in and then realized your flight had been delayed, so I waited," he says as he reaches out to take my carry-on from me.

I let him because this isn't a fight I have the energy for.

"Let me get you home so you can sleep. You look like hell," he says.

"Gee, thanks, the words every girl longs to hear." I roll my eyes and head off to get my bags.

I know he has to be as tired as I am, but he still takes care of me, grabbing my bags and getting us to his car.

"How is your car here?" I ask.

"After I saw your flight was delayed, I had a buddy drop it off this morning." He shrugs like it's no big deal, but it is a big deal. Though I see his bags are already here, so he's been here for a while.

When I get in the car, he makes sure my seat-belt is buckled before fighting airport traffic.

It's all too familiar being in a car with him.

"When was the last time you ate?" he asks.

"I have no damn clue. Denver, I think. Somewhere between the first and second delay."

He stops at a fast food place and grabs breakfast for both of us.

"Eat," he orders.

"I don't want to eat in your car."

While I don't know much about cars, this one looks expensive, and it's kept immaculate. There isn't a speck of dust or dirt, nothing out of place.

"I don't care about the car. I care about you, now eat, baby girl." His tone is stern but soft, and when my stomach grumbles, giving me away. I finally devour my breakfast sandwich and hash browns.

"Thank you," I tell him and make sure to clean up as much of the crumbs as I can.

Now that my belly is full and I'm at a place I feel safe, I've hit a wall. My eyes get heavy, and West must notice I'm fighting to keep them open.

"It's okay, get some sleep. I'll take care of you." He rests his hand on my arm.

Despite everything that has happened, I still feel safe with him because I know he will take care of me, if for no other reason than because I'm Nate's little sister.

Even as I close my eyes, my brain is at war with my heart, telling it that isn't the only reason he's taking of me.

What's that famous saying? 'I'll worry about it tomorrow.'

Chapter 15

Weston

She was so tired she fell asleep as soon as she finished eating. Probably for the best, because I had planned to bring her to my place so I could take care of her. After the night she's had, she needs some pampering.

I carefully pick her up and carry her into my house, and lay her in my bed. Then I go get our bags. Walking into my room and seeing her lying in my bed, my soul settles for the first time since we watched the sunset on the beach the night before we got to the wedding.

This is right. So, I waste no time unpacking my stuff and hers. Then I place her bathroom items in with mine and take a photo. I don't know why, but seeing her stuff mixed with mine is just as sexy as seeing her lying in my bed.

Then going to my office, I pull out a spare house key and look for her keys in her purse. After placing my house key on her key ring, I crawl into bed with her. Carefully though, so

I don't wake her up, I pull her against me and simply hold her.

I don't know how long I hold her, but the hours pass from midmorning, and I drift off and wake every time she moves. When the sun starts to set, she rolls over again and wakes me this time. A minute later, she wakes, and her eyes lock on mine.

She doesn't ask where we are, just trusts me, and neither of us says a word. Staring into her eyes is intense, and the need to kiss her is so strong. I slowly lean down toward her, giving her time to stop me, which I'm sure she will.

When she doesn't stop me and my lips land on hers, I can't stop the moan that comes from me. She kisses me back. The kiss is heated and passionate, and I want nothing more than to take it further. Instead, I pull back because I need her to know.

"It's always been you. The first time I saw you was on the playground at school, and you were following Nate around. Your hair was in pigtails, and you wore jeans and the Disney Princess shirt you loved."

"You remember that?" she asks in awe.

"Every detail. That Christmas of my senior year when we spent it together at the cabin with your parents and Nate's girlfriend? I can't remember a better Christmas. You always seemed to smell of sugar cookies and peppermint and would wear those oversized sweaters and leggings. At night we'd watch a movie, and you would fall asleep on my shoulder before we even got halfway through. I'd stay up and hold you and watch the movie, then carry you to bed like I did today."

I gently kiss her forehead.

"I'm not going to be with anyone else. Only you."

Her eyes mist over, and I lean in to give her a chaste kiss.

"You hungry?" She nods.

"Where are we?"

"My place. Why don't you take a shower, and I'll make us dinner?"

Going into the kitchen, I check what food I have in the freezer since I've been gone for two weeks. When I dig through it, I find some pizzas, so I go to my bedroom to see if that's ok with her.

I find Rory standing in the bathroom, just staring at her stuff mixed in with mine.

"Why?" She wants to know, and I could play dumb and pretend I won't know what she means, but I have the answer, so I tell her truthfully.

"When I realized there was nothing I could say to fix this, I knew I had to prove to you I'm in this and that I pick this, us, you. I pick you, and I'm going to show you. I've never lived with anyone, but I want you here. Even if we're fighting and I'm sleeping on the couch, I want you here."

Taking a deep breath, I decide to go all in. This wasn't how I planned it, but I can't seem to stop it.

"I love you, Rory, and I'm going to show you every day. Move in with me and let me make it up to you."

She starts shaking her head, but I stop her.

"If I don't make this work, and if I don't prove to you, I'm all in, then I'll move you anywhere you want to go and pay a year's rent."

Her eyes go wide, and I can't blame her because this is a huge deal but one I'm more than ready for.

"Okay," she says.

She agreed.

She's going to move in, and I'll see her every day. But more than that, it means she's willing to give me a second chance. I'm not going to waste it, and I'll prove to her and others that there will not be any regrets.

Then I pull her into my arms and enjoy the feeling of her being in my arms. She melts into me, and the thought of pushing my luck and climbing into the shower with her crosses my mind, but I won't screw this up. Slow and steady.

"I don't have much for food. Though I have some frozen pizzas, or I can call for takeout." I say, reluctantly pulling away from her.

"Pizza actually sounds good."

"Okay, take a shower, and I'll get it going."

Back in the kitchen, I get the pizzas baking and then start looking up moving companies. I want her in here as soon as possible. No chance for her to change her mind.

When she walks out of the bedroom with her hair wet and wearing nothing but one of my oversized shirts, I'm instantly hard.

"You have never looked more beautiful." Her cheeks turn red with my words.

Taking a seat at the kitchen island, she watches me as I pull out plates and cups for us to use.

"I found a company that can move your stuff the day after tomorrow. They do all the packing and everything. Just let me know what furniture I need to make room for."

She shakes her head.

"You don't do anything slowly, do you?"

"Well, I do one thing slow when asked." I slide my hand up her thigh and find she is wearing nothing but a pair of panties under the shirt. My groan is involuntary.

Pure torture.

***

Rory

West wasn't joking about moving me in as soon as possible. By the time I got to call Kinsley to give her an update, I was moved in, and she demanded to come over. Then she spent the day helping me unpack, interrogating me, and demanding answers more effectively than any cop could ever do.

Then she sent West across town to get food so she could talk about sex. Even though Kinsley is my friend, and I share just about everything with her, there were a few things I kept to myself.

By the end of the day, she gave the move her blessing with some direct threats to West's manhood if he screwed up again.

Today, we're getting ready for my brother and Mandy to visit. I'm fully unpacked, but we haven't told them I moved in with West. When we had my parents over three nights ago, we asked them not to tell him either. They agreed so long as we do it tonight.

I'm making my brother's favorite blueberry cheesecake, and West is grilling steaks for dinner.

When strong arms wrap around me from behind, I realize how much I've zoned out.

As West nuzzles my neck, he whispers. "Everything is going to be fine. You'll see. And if he doesn't approve, screw him. Because you're here, you are mine, and I pick you. I'll always pick you."

Though we haven't had sex since I moved in, West has been loving and affectionate. While he can't keep his hands off me, and he cuddles with me every chance get gets. Oh, he'll give me multiple orgasms, but won't let me touch him.

"You know," I say, turning and running my hand over his cock, "we have time to have some fun."

"You want to cum, baby girl?" West kisses my neck.

"Always, but you need to cum more."

"Don't worry about me, let me focus on you."

I slap his chest, not hard, but enough to get his attention.

"Of course, I worry about you. What kind of girlfriend would I be if I didn't? Please tell me why you won't take this any further. Is it because you are still waiting on Nate's approval of me living here?"

"Fuck no. Please tell me that's not what you have been thinking."

"Of course, that's what I have been thinking! You won't tell me why you just distract me with your amazingly talented tongue."

He smirks for a fraction of a second before his face goes serious again.

"I want to prove myself to you. That I pick *you*, not Nate or your parents. Also, I need you to forgive me for being an idiot in Napa, and I don't ever want to take advantage of you. So, until you forgive me, and you know without a shadow of a doubt that I'm in this, on your side, then I don't cum. Not by your hand or mine."

"West..." We are interrupted by a knock on the door.

He leans in, gives me a quick kiss, and reaches down to adjust himself before answering the door.

Nate and Mandy walk in, and of course, they're early.

Mandy comes right to me and gives me a huge hug.

"Look at you!" I say. "You're glowing. Italy agrees with you."

"That's what Nate said. He kept trying to buy a villa while we were there to convince me to go back more."

I lower my voice, "Depending on how today goes, I might insist on your taking him up on it and moving him over there permanently."

Hugging Mandy again, I then walk over to West's side, where he and my brother seem to be having some kind of stare-off. The moment I'm at West's side, he pushes me to stand behind him. While I love his protective side, I think he's the one who needs protecting.

"Let's just tell them and get this over with," I sigh.

"Tell me what?" Nate grits out.

Mandy walks to his side and grips his arm, and Nate pushes her behind him in the same move West did to me. I peek out from behind West's back to find Mandy peeking out from behind Nate.

"West and I moved in together," I say, ripping off the Band-Aid.

"Moving a little fast, aren't you?" my brother asks.

"Really, Nate? Do we not remember Diamond?"

"Yeah, and look how that turned out."

"Who's Diamond?" Mandy asks.

"No one," Nate says, and Mandy glares at me. The mention of a name she doesn't know means she wants the details, and she isn't going to drop this.

I mouth 'later' to her, and she nods.

"Rory is no Diamond, and you know it. Saying she is going to pull that stunt is an insult to her." West's voice is low and calm but pretty freakin' scary.

"What stunt?" Mandy asks, throwing her arms in the air.

Nate looks like he is going to murder West, so I decide to take some of that anger and let him focus on me. Why? I have no idea.

"Diamond is a stripper Nate met at a strip club. She gave him this sob story, and he moved her in with him two weeks after meeting her. A month later, he came home from work, and she had cleared his apartment out, quit her job, and fled, after also draining him of a few thousand dollars."

Nate's eyes never move from West.

"Outside." Nate grits out, and West nods.

"So, help me, Nate, if you hurt him, don't bother coming back in here!" I yell after them before Nate slams the door behind him.

Mandy and I look at each other then race to the front window, kneeling on the couch and not even bothering to hide. We are avidly watching what they're going to do.

They stand in the front yard staring at each other.

"Dammit, I can't hear. How do you open these windows?" Mandy asks.

"Hell, if I know, I just moved in." Then out of nowhere, Nate takes a swing at West. It's so sudden I let out a scream and cringe. West takes it like it's nothing. I guess it helps West has a good three inches on Nate and about fifty pounds of muscle.

West doesn't swing back, but Nate swings again, and even Mandy grimaces this time. West takes the hit, but on the third, West stops him and pins him to the tree behind him.

"Dammit, still can't hear them," I say, pressing my ear to the window.

A moment later, West steps back and turns to come inside. By the time they both walk in the door, it's like nothing happened.

Later that night, lying in bed, I have to know.

"What did you say to Nate when you had him pressed to the tree?"

West looks over at me hesitantly, but I know he'll tell me since I asked a direct question. I take his hand in mine and kiss it, reminding him I'm here, and I'm his.

"I told him one swing was for not talking to him before we started dating, and one was for moving you in here without telling him. Then I reminded him I was bigger than him and I could protect you better than he ever could. I told him friend or not he takes another swing at me in my house, I would return it. That's the clean version of it."

"Amazing what gets accomplished when one man hits another," I sigh.

Nate walked out of here tonight all smiles and happy for us. But that still hasn't changed West's policy that it goes no further than making me cum.

I need a new game plan.

Chapter 16

Weston

After dinner with Nate and Mandy last night, I wanted to take her out on a date, and she agreed. Though she tried to cancel this morning when she saw the bruises on my ribs from where Nate punched me. But I assured her I was fine, and after she kissed every inch of every bruise, she agreed we could still go out today.

So here we are walking along the Chicago River, taking in the beautiful day. She's holding my hand with a smile on her face, and she looks so damn beautiful.

"Have you ever done one of the boat rides down the river?" I ask her.

"No, you'd think living here that I would have by now."

"I haven't either. What would you think about doing one?"

"Great idea! I'd like that."

Let me tell you, there is nothing like holding my girl in my arms as she leans into me while we enjoy a boat ride. This is the best way to say she's mine while she's cuddling with me, and it's my arms around her. It's certainly soothing, for sure.

About midway through the ride, a couple a few rows in front of us catch our attention, and a moment later, the guy drops to one knee and proposes. When she says yes, the whole boat erupts, clapping, cheering, and congratulating.

Everyone can't take their eyes off the couple, but my eyes go to Rory. Her beautiful face is lit up in pure happiness for some strangers. But when she turns that smile on me, I feel like I won the lottery.

"I love you, West." When I hear those words, I swear I swallow my tongue. My heart feels like it's about to burst from my chest.

"I was hurt," she goes on, "but I think that I was looking for a reason to push you away because I was scared. I'm so sorry I hurt you. But you didn't run, and that says everything to me." Before I can say anything, she pulls me down for a kiss.

This kiss may be simple, but it's the most important kiss of my life. So, I take control of it and show her everything she means to me with my kiss.

For the rest of the boat ride, we make out like teenagers, unable to keep our hands off each other. Finally, we cut the date short and head back to the house.

Once there, I sit her on the couch.

"Wait here," I say, and she nods, so I disappear into the bedroom to get the gift I've been holding on to for a while now.

When I'm right in front of her, I drop down to one knee and open the square velvet box.

"It was the day we were in Santa Monica, and Kinsley called you. I went window shopping hoping to find a ring. This was in the window, and it screamed you. Even though you were mad at me, I wanted to ask you to marry me at Nate's reception. But you snuck out. When we got home, I thought we'd move slowly as I was attempting to show you that I would always pick you."

Taking the ring from the box, I hold it in front of her. "I wasn't entirely truthful with you yesterday when you asked me what I said to Nate when I had him pressed to the tree. I also told him I was going to marry you as soon as I could get you to say yes. Then I told him his opinion didn't matter, but for your sake, he better support the day."

"That's why he walked in smiling?" She asks in a shaky voice.

"Yeah, I guess he realized how serious I was. But hearing you say you loved me today, well, it's like my world finally shifted into focus. I'll wait until the end of time for you if that is what you want, but I don't want to wait any longer to start our life together. You are already moved in, now I'm asking you to be my wife. Let me love you, let me show you every day you will always come first, in more ways than one." I smirk at the double meaning, and her cheeks flush.

"Will you marry me, be my wife, and let me love you, support you, and take care of you for the rest of my life?"

She is silent for a moment, and while her eyes have misted over, she doesn't say and word, and my heart drops. Maybe I misread the whole day. My mouth goes dry, and I am about to stand up when she leans down and kisses me. It's a soft, sweet kiss, and before I can deepen it, she pulls away.

"When I was nine, I roped you and Nate into playing wedding with me. Remember? I married you, and Nate was the minister?"

Damn, how did I forget that?

"You wore your Easter dress. It was pale pink, and your mom did your hair up with a wild-flower crown."

She nods with a smile lighting up her face. "I knew then I wanted to marry you, even if I didn't understand it. As I grew up, I thought it was just a silly little girl notion. But sitting here today, I know there is nothing I want more than to be your wife. Yes, I'll marry you."

I don't think there are words to describe the overwhelming pure happiness that floods my body. My hands shake as I slide the ring onto her finger. The moment I place it there, I bring her hand to my mouth and kiss the inside of her palm.

She launches herself into me and wraps her arms around my neck and her legs around my waist. "Does this mean you will finally make love to me again?" she whispers against my ear as I stand up.

"I need to be inside you like I need my last breath. I love you, baby girl."

"I love you too, West. Always."

Epilogue 1

Rory

Six Months Later

I look at the clock and then call Nate.

"Are you almost here?" I ask him.

"Tomorrow night. You had it right. This road trip thing is a blast," Nate says with a smile in his voice.

Strong arms wrap around me from behind, and I lean into my West. We're getting married next weekend, and Nate and Mandy decided to road trip Route 66 from California to Chicago. Of course, they were supposed to be here three days ago.

"Okay, well, if you aren't here tomorrow y'all are sleeping on the floor because I'm giving your room to Kinsley."

"Doesn't she have her own place?"

"Yes, but she wants to be close for wedding planning. She's taking the couch, but if you aren't here, then your bed is fair game."

We've set up the guest bedroom for Nate and Mandy anytime they want to visit. Since visiting after their honeymoon, they have been here twice. It was awkward the first time, but we got over it fast.

"Text me when you stop tonight," I say before hanging up.

West turns me in his arms, so I'm facing him on his lap. We just sit and be for a few minutes while it's quiet. We both know tomorrow the wedding week chaos starts.

"What do you think our wedding drama will be?" I ask since it seems to be a family tradition. I guess at Mom and Dad's wedding they found the best man and maid of honor getting it on in the bridal suite. The problem was they were both married to someone else. So, a little wedding theatrics has become our family's custom.

"Besides not getting you down the aisle fast enough?" West says, and I know he is only partly joking.

"Besides that." I kiss his cheek.

"Probably my aunt hitting on your dad."

West's Aunt Jilly has a thing for married men and could care less about their wives. She hits on them relentlessly, and the last time she hit on my dad, my mom went off on her. That was at West's high school graduation.

I had never seen that side of my mom before or since, but let's just say I had to use headphones that night because they fought horizontally, if you know what I mean. Things kids should never know about their parents.

"Well, if it's a repeat of last time, it sure will be entertaining. Need to tell Nate to make sure to record it," I chuckle.

"I can't wait to marry you," he mumbles before carrying me to bed to show me how much.

***

Weston

We did it. We're married. I can't believe it. This amazingly beautiful girl that I've had a crush on my whole life is now my wife.

My Wife.

I don't think I'll ever tire of saying that. As I watch her and Nate on the dance floor, all I can think about is how I can't wait to get her back to our room tonight. She's had a permanent smile on her face and looks so beautiful in the lace wedding dress that hugs her every curve. As for

me, my dick has been hard since the moment
we said I do.

When the song ends, I stand and make my
way to her, pulling her into my arms. Nate gives
me a knowing smile, and almost right on time,
Rory's mother's voice fills the air.

"Did you not learn your lesson last time, you
old hag? Lay another finger on my husband,
and I'll chop it off."

We all turn to look and find she has a steak
knife in her hand.

"Not again," Nate groans. I just look at Rory,
and we both start laughing.

"Well, if you could satisfy him in bed, he
wouldn't be looking my way." Aunt Jilly says,
and the entire room gasps.

"You take your mom, and I'll get my aunt," I
say to Nate, who nods, and we start to make our
way across the room.

Then her dad chimes in. "Trust me, I didn't
look at you. I don't do older women, and my
wife is more in bed than I can handle."

"Fuck. Things you don't need to know about
your parents." Nate says as we are fighting our
way through the crowd that is gathered around
the table.

When we finally break through, I step in front
of my aunt at the same time my dad walks up
behind her.

"Jill, this is why no one invites you to anything anymore." My dad growls at his sister.

"It's time for her to go home," I tell my dad, who nods wearily.

"I got her." He takes her hand, and Aunt Jilly follows. She always trusts her brother and would follow him anywhere. But she turns one last time and gives what I'm sure she thinks is a flirtatious smirk at Nate's dad.

Once my aunt is out of the room, Rory bursts out laughing, and slowly the room follows suit.

"How was that for wedding drama, Mom?" Rory asks.

Her mom glares at her but then turns to hide a smile. We hurry through the cake cutting and saying our goodbyes as we race to our room. We're staying at the same hotel where the wedding is being held. Tomorrow we leave for our honeymoon.

Nate paid for the entire honeymoon, saying he owed us that much. It's a trip to Greece and Spain. The top two countries on Rory's out-of--the-country bucket list. I can't wait to explore them with her.

Once in the room, I turn and pin her to the back of the door.

"Your signature move." She says, smiling.

"What?"

She laughs, "It started when we were driving Route 66. We'd get to our room, and you'd turn and pin me to the back of the door. It's your signature move, and I love it." She pulls me in for a kiss.

"Guess I hadn't realized I was doing it so much. But it's because once we're alone, I can't wait to get my hands and lips on you," I tell her just before my lips land on hers.

We make out for a few minutes with her pressed to the door as I run my hands over every inch of her I can touch.

"Now, how do we get this dress off of you? Because it's too nice to just rip in half."

"Don't you dare!" she gasps.

I wouldn't because she looks too good to ruin it, and I already have fantasies of her wearing this dress a few years down the road for me to recreate this night.

"Get on the bed, wife," I growl as soon as the dress slips from her body.

"I hope you didn't plan on getting any sleep tonight."

She giggles, and I swear it's the sweetest sound in the world. "No plans whatsoever."

"Good."

Because I plan to spend every day of our forever making her cum over and over again.

***

Want a bonus epilogue of West and Rory? **<u>Sign up for my newsletter</u>** to get a free bonus epilogue set five years later!

Want to know more about Walker Lake and Ben's friends? Check out **The Cowboy and His Everything**, read it for free!

More Books By Kaci Rose

See all of Kaci Rose's Books

Oakside Military Heroes Series

Saving Noah – Lexi and Noah

Saving Easton – Easton and Paisley

Saving Teddy – Teddy and Mia

Saving Levi – Levi and Mandy

Saving Gavin – Gavin and Lauren

Mountain Men of Whiskey River

Take Me To The River – Axel and Emelie

Take Me To The Cabin – Pheonix and Jenna

Take Me To The Lake – Cash and Hope

Take Me To The Mountain – Bennett and Willow

Chasing the Sun Duet

Sunrise – Kade and Lin

Sunset – Jasper and Brynn

Rock Stars of Nashville

She's Still The One – Dallas and Austin

Standalone Books

Texting Titan - Denver and Avery

Accidental Sugar Daddy – Owen and Ellie

Saving Mason - Mason and Paige

Stay With Me Now – David and Ivy

Midnight Rose - Ruby and Orlando

Committed Cowboy – Whiskey Run Cowboys

Billionaire's Marigold

Stalking His Obsession - Dakota and Grant

Connect with Kaci Rose

Website

Facebook

Kaci Rose Reader's Facebook Group

TikTok

Instagram

Twitter

Goodreads

Book Bub

Join Kaci Rose's VIP List (Newsletter)

About Kaci Rose

Kaci Rose writes steamy contemporary romance mostly set in small towns. She grew up in Florida but longs for the mountains over the beach.
She is a mom to 5 kids and a dog who is scared of his own shadow.

She also writes steamy cowboy romance as Kaci M. Rose.

Please Leave a Review!

I love to hear from my readers! Please **head over to your favorite store and leave a review** of what you thought of this book!

Made in the USA
Columbia, SC
24 September 2024

42937631R00104